W9-CIB-173

SEMAPHORE

Also by G. W. Hawkes

Surveyor
Playing Out of the Deep Woods
Spies in the Blue Smoke

Semaphore

G. W. Hawkes

MacMurray & Beck
Denver

Published by:
MacMurray & Beck
1649 Downing St.
Denver, CO 80218

Printed and bound in the United States of America

2 3 4 5 6 7 8 9 10

Library of Congress Cataloging-in-Publication Data
Hawkes, G. W., 1953–
Semaphore: a novel / G. W. Hawkes.
p. cm.
ISBN 1-878448-82-X (hardcover)
I. Title.
PS3558.A818S45 1998
813′.54—dc21 97-46687
CIP

MacMurray & Beck Fiction: General Editor, Greg Michalson
Semaphore cover design by Laurie Dolphin,
interior design by Stacia Schaefer.
The text was set in Weiss by Chris Davis, Mulberry Tree Enterprises.

Publisher's Note: This is a work of fiction. Names, characters, places, and incidents either are the product of the author's imagination or are used fictitiously. Any resemblance to actual events, locales, or persons, living or dead, is entirely coincidental.

for Steven Oliver Tharp,

a friend who died twenty years ago attempting
to rescue a drowning dog in Bakersfield, California

It's a pleasure to be able to thank a few people in print: my wife, Kay, for her continuous help and understanding, and her help in my understanding of these characters, particularly Luce; my friends and colleagues Dr. Sascha Feinstein and Dr. David Rife for their meticulous editing (I should thank Sascha twice); Vicki Strong for reading and Dr. John Whelan for listening; my colleagues Dr. Michelle Briggs (biology), Dr. David Fisher (physics), Dr. Kathleen D. Pagana (nursing), and Dr. Gene Sprechini (mathematics), for answering questions that at the moment, wanting answers, would have slowed the manuscript, and Judge Tom Raup for a line over coffee one morning that I simply stole; the colleagues in my department who left me alone to write it, and Lycoming College for a semester's sabbatical leave to get it started; and most of all, my editor, Greg Michalson, for making me make this book what it should be. Thank you.

And summer mornings the mute child, rebellious,
Stupid, hating the words, the meanings, hating
The Think now, Think, the Oh but Think! would leave

Archibald MacLeish, "Eleven"

Side by side the houses rise from dirt-hard lots in stuccoed oblongs and low, upright, flattened squares to lean against one another so close the red tiles of their roofs crawl and hump and seethe. Windows at odd angles in the light look like unfinished parts in a painting, Joseph thinks, or the transparent creamy bits in his kaleidoscope. Sidewalks in long curves end in cul-de-sacs, flat until the coming earthquake buckles them. But first these growing giant-rooted trees will be pushed over by bulldozers.

The boy pulled the whistle on its cord from his pocket where he'd put it climbing up so it wouldn't snag and hung it again around his neck. His chrome-plated larynx. It could warble, whistle, shrill, but couldn't speak. He tapped it with a thumbnail, and the shriveled pea in it rattled. He tapped his own throat.

Other boys spring up from the ground like promises and ride bright bikes in tight and tighter spirals, calling and waving and flashing the secret hand signals of summer. Joseph's hand closed on the braided cord as if he could pull them closer with a tug. This, too, one day, perhaps.

At dawn the dark ghosts of not-yet-dead trees were pulled back into the ground by their roots, the shiny black leaves against his face greening and clattering. A bird asked a question and then: day for real and the machinery snorted and hard-hatted men called to each other but couldn't be heard.

Joseph's tree was circled with an orange ribbon because he'd tied it there. He'd sentenced another, smaller one in stealing this, and his guilt was as real as when he pictures his little sister dead. (She'll give up all her air in a neighbor's swimming pool in three years and a month and he is helpless to stop it, as orange ribbons can't be tied around sisters. But his parents in one grieving, mindless, im- and unpassioned mechanical moment will make another child, a brother, Louis, after her.) He caught the glint of its color like sunset on the horizon of his lower eyelid, and he took the whistle into his mouth and blew a long, shallow, lung-emptying regret.

For him, beginnings had their endings planted in them. When he was younger, his father had tried to show him the Bear and the Bull and the Archer, but he couldn't connect the dots in the sky—not even the Dippers—because for him the stars had moved somewhere into the future. But it wouldn't have mattered; even when he saw the constellations in picture books, they looked nothing like what they were supposed to, and he knew that others (not others, everybody) thought so too, and he wondered why civilization held on to pictures that made no sense. Our boy, his father told his mother while looking up from his book, is outside sidereal time. Mother laughed, as if she didn't believe it, as if by laughing they could pretend otherwise for another day, even though every mismatched moment of their lives was another proof they couldn't.

His parents would sometimes inexplicably age: at the breakfast table or in front of the television his father's bald head gleams like hard pink plastic, and more and more often now his mother skids into a sunny late afternoon she hasn't lived through yet and sits in her chair by the window, her head a cloud, and dozes because she has breaths left in her she no longer wants. But he never sees his father alone in that distant not-yet, and Louise never grows older than six.

He can point out coming collisions (fender-benders, hurricanes), but he's been spared so far living the tedious moments of his own future more than the once he has coming. Each new doctor with still another test, another probe and theory, another attempt to map his missing voice, would be unbearable repeated. *God watches.* What remained the same for him as if he'd lived it before were the shrugs after. "He has the necessary machinery," one said (they all said). "It just isn't working."

Joseph turned back to this more real now with an effort, his nose close against the sinus-searing bark of the sweetgum that made his head light. He peeled a page of it and rolled it in a fist.

A circle of yellow machines unwound like metal thread from an invisible spool and darted or lumbered, each to its task, into Joseph's birthright. He clapped his hands over his ears against the labored coughs and metal-shearing screams of those tracked tons, and against the clouds of dirt that hummed and shimmered with the invisible beat of giant insect wings, and against the gunshots of felled trees. One after another, the sweetgums and live oaks—and the sycamores, two at a time—were pushed down. Something quick and brown and frightened was plowed under. Joseph sees like an afterimage the flat, blurry shape of Louise at the bottom of the pool that isn't even a hole yet.

Men appeared like those not-quite-imaginary future boys, but these held real chains with real hooks that flashed, dangling, from gloved hands. Quick, calf-roping, they wrapped each splintered bole and dragged it off, leaving a mangle of limbs in a scar behind. Dump trucks—Diamond Reos—carried red soil from one place to another and left their loads in long, low mounds. Joseph's vision could not see backward, but nevertheless he recognized cemeteries and battlefields.

By dusk the naked ground was nearly level, all the trees but a couple of dozen gone. The new open spaces collected piles of horizontal trees, and then like signal fires the piles were lit, fueled by old tires and the hot air blown in by fans. This raised new, sooty clouds just as the old ones were finally settling. His parents walked through the smoke. His mother called. His father. From his left and right, they quartered the slaughtered place—

"Joseph!"

"Joseph Carl Taft!"

"Where are you, Joseph?"

—his father the harmony, his mother the melody.

They came together in the exact center, a three-stranded knot with the man who'd been left behind to keep an eye on the burning. His mother kept raising her fingers to her mouth and then spreading them, and Joseph knew what she was saying: he's mute; he can't speak (she always said it both ways, and with her hands too, as if her listeners not only couldn't comprehend but couldn't hear); then father-mother-nightwatch untangled themselves to crouch, look with hands raised against the heat into the red hearts of the smoldering piles for a scrap of jeans or a pair of smoking tennis shoes.

She'd have the police here soon if they weren't already coming. Joseph shinnied from his hiding place and blew his whistle: You needn't worry about me, Mother; here I am. She ran to him, hugged him, then pushed him back and cuffed the back of his head. Then hugged him again. His father stuck fists into his pockets.

He was sent to his room.

"My hair's going gray."

"You're too young for that."

"You can't see them in the blonde ones, but they're there."

"He's a boy."

"He is, Frank. A boy with a disability. Maybe two."

"He's a boy," his father repeated, and raised his hands and shrugged. They'd both gotten into the habit. "You can't put a boy within hearing distance of big yellow machines and not want him to look."

"Look?"

"That's all he was doing."

"Looking from the top of a tree they might have pushed down." She stood up, to be the tree. "And what chance does a boy have who can't speak?"

He's got the whistle, his father almost said.

"And a boy who's not even in the right time. God knows *when* he was. For all we know he didn't see the bulldozers, but a playground or a park—"

"Helen."

"Or a *pond*," she said, picturing him suddenly and illogically up to his waist in dirt. "Don't you dare Helen me."

He was beaten, mostly because he felt the same way, and what was worse, she knew it. He cradled his chin in the heels of his hands, and finally she let the rest of her air out and sat.

"Well?"

"You're right," he said. "But you've never been a boy."

"Don't give me that. Your never having been a girl hasn't stopped you from being a father to Louise."

"Not yet."

She raised an eyebrow, the left one.

It worked on him as effectively as it did on her son. "I always figured, when she got older, when she began dating—I don't know."

"That you'd leave the dirty work to me."

He nodded, guilty.

"And how old is Joseph," she said quietly, "when I bow out?"

"Helen—"

"You know," she said, "I'm almost willing to do that, at some point. I guess I'll *have* to, at some point. God knows half the world treats the other half as if we've got a codebook and a radio set. But Frank, he's got to somehow live long enough for the two of you to go off into the woods alone, or down to the basement, or up in a treehouse, or wherever."

He nodded, not looking at her.

"That's our job now, Frank: to worry about Joseph."

"All right, yes. But we can't hold him too tight. He's got to breathe."

She put her hands on her chest, one on top of each breast, spreading her fingers. "Is that what I'm doing? Squeezing the air out of him?"

"I don't know, Helen."

"Tell me if I am."

"I don't know." His right hand came off his lap as if lifted by a string, then fell back. He stared at it instead of her. "He's already a prisoner of the future."

"I see."

"I didn't mean it to sound like that."

"No?"

"No. I just meant—hell, what did I mean? He's seen us die."

Her hand went to her throat.

"Well, he must've. And who knows what else? I guess what I'm saying is that he's more grown up than his age. He blew his whistle when he saw us looking for him. He treats Louise with real tenderness lately. He does his homework without us asking. He's old for eleven."

"Ten."

"Fine, ten. Eleven in a couple of weeks. He's probably older than us in some ways. You and I both know he's lived some of our future already."

"What are you saying?"

"Maybe he knows what hurts him and what doesn't."

She stared at her husband for a long minute and then left the room. *Oh, Christ,* he thought, but she came back towing Joseph in his pajamas and had him sit between them on the couch.

"You had us worried, honey," she said.

Joseph nodded quickly, before she was finished.

She patted his hand. Slow down. "Your dad thinks that maybe you know when you're safe or not."

He nodded again, quickly.

"Is that true?"

Another nod.

"Truthfully? Not just thinking you're safe, but knowing it?"

A slower nod that stopped. And then a small shake of his head.

"You haven't seen—what?—help me, Frank."

"Joseph," his father said, "have you ever seen the end of your own future?"

Joseph shook his head.

Have you seen mine? he wanted to ask. "That's a dangerous place, all those machines."

Joseph opened the fingers on one hand. I know.

"Dangerous for a boy who *can* talk."

His son smiled, thanking him for that.

"A voice or a whistle, either one, probably couldn't be heard in all that racket."

Joseph touched his shoulders with both hands. They can see *me*.

"In a tree?"

He smiled again, sheepishly, then nodded, agreeing not with the question but with the unsaid answer.

"You'll watch from the edges, out in the open?"

He nodded. And then, to his father's horror, Joseph leaped from the couch to embrace him. The boy's knee caught him in the groin. *Oh, God,* Frank's eyes asked Helen, *what does he know?*

He didn't do what he'd promised, but almost. *Almost* should get half credit. Boys are natural lawyers, and when he'd seen the loophole in front of him the night before, he'd agreed with his father with mental fingers loosely crossed. A construction site has lots of edges, and one of them is the place they've already been.

The new ground was hard and flat as a parking lot, bumpy with raw white roots like bones in it. Joseph blinked away the next image that wanted to come—others always watching, perhaps from other times, as he did—and concentrated instead on the smells that held him in the now: bleeding wood, dirt like sugar, the cloying clot of diesel.

A boy not much older than he crouched on a machine's slick yellow hood, taking the measure of its fuel with a yardstick. He screwed the cap back on and slid off. Joseph fingered his whistle but didn't blow it. A pickup rattled at him, then past, the windows, even the windshield, so streaked with mud he couldn't see the men inside.

The tree piles smoked. He catches a breath of autumn in a place he's never been. A snowflake settles on his nose in a memory he doesn't have. A woman stands in a doorway warm with buttery light and calls to him. *Joe.*

Wife? Daughter? He rubs a hand down a jean-clad thigh as if he can read his age in it and raises a hand in answer.

Bring the wood.

He's holding an ax in that upraised hand.

"This ain't school, kid. What'ya wan' say?"

Joseph stared at the man, at his suddenly empty hand, and lowered both his eyes and his arm.

"You're that deaf kid, ain't you? The one can't speak. The one his mother was lookin' for last night."

Joseph nodded, flicked his ear with a finger. I'm not deaf.

"She thought maybe you was in a pile." The man's eyebrows came together. "Told her that hardly ever happens." Haw haw haw.

They stared at each other, Joseph wanting to run.

"So, what'ya wan' say? An' how you goin' to say it?"

Joseph thought about motioning the man over, having him bend close, and then breaking his eardrum with the whistle.

"You want to ride on the machines, huh? Kids do."

Joseph nodded before thinking, realizing at the same time that it was exactly what he wanted.

"Come on, then." But he held a hand up, stopping Joseph before he'd taken a step. The two middle fingers were splayed, like blister swellings, missing their tips. "When you're not holdin' on, keep your hands in close."

I will.

They called it a loader. Tank tracks instead of wheels. A big, toothed, clamshelled bucket out front could have carried four grown men. Its job was to push the piles together, mix in the air and spark them up again, and set them going.

A belch of engine smoke through the trees warned Joseph in time for him to turn and see the red elbow of an excavator dip up and swivel, and he hoped the man he was riding with would go that way.

"Hang on, now. Here." Joseph had a sidesaddle seat on the hollow toolchest arm of the driver's chair, and it must have been built for kids because everywhere in reach was something to hang on to. The man pushed two levers forward and the loader jerked into motion, and then he pulled one back with an index finger, reversing a tread, and the machine spun 360 degrees and the man laughed. "Yee, haw."

As he'd suspected, they were only bigger kids.

They drove into the fires, and the new flames licked over the bucket and the tree-sulphurous smoke boiled out around the loader and when he closed his eyes to its sting he saw that woman waiting for him, for the wood, but this time it was memory of the time before and nothing else. Sometime, though, he'd have to use that ax and carry in the wood. Not yet. There was all the time in the world to meet the girl and be a husband and hardly any time at all to be ten.

Pushing stumps, carrying gravel, they circumnavigated the new plat at a mile an hour, the driver pointing out streets and houses to come, although Joseph, with his gift, pointed first almost every time. He would have told the man, if he'd been able, the names of the families moving into those invisible homes, what cars they drove, their children's names.

At lunch the man tried to find a hard hat to fit him, but even after cinching down the plastic web inside he couldn't do it. He stuffed one with a stocking cap and a pair of socks and slapped it onto Joseph crookedly. "Wear that. OSHA'd have our ass."

"Have it anyway," another man said, then smiled to take the barb out. "Boss'll do it for 'em, probably."

"Yeah." He looked at Joseph. "Yeah," he said again. "I guess that's right. But we had a good ride, huh?"

Joseph nodded.

"Sort of illegal."

"Stupid," said the other man. "Insurance. Or the kid's mother."

"I guess, kid, that was it."

Joseph nodded again. He wanted to watch the big red hoe digging anyway. The man handed him a cheese sandwich as a consolation prize, and he ate it, as happy as he could ever remember being.

The ditch wasn't as long as he'd hoped, but it was deeper: three times a man's height and fifty feet long. One end got covered up while the other got dug out, so the slick white pipe slid through the ground like a snake. He wanted to go down in it, but he knew not to ask. The pipelayer signaled the machine in front of him and the machine behind him and the men on top with the pipe when he wanted more dirt moved, more ditch filled, more pipe or gravel. The thick plastic sang when they dropped it in and covered it with pea gravel the way railroad tracks will if you skip a rock across them. A laser beam for grade inside the pipe turned the dust clouds redder and wavered like a bull's-eye on the man's ankle.

He watched at the end of the day as they planted a manhole, hoisting the concrete rings with chains and hooks, and then he sat with them on the pickup's tailgate and listened to their stories of how the day had gone. He handed out beers from their ice chests when they wanted them, and he watched them drive away. All that showed of the day's work were some steel lids on top of the dirt, but now he knew the ground was hollow everywhere, and not just the place Louise would find.

"Have fun?" his father asked.

He must be able to see that.

"Stay out of the way?"

Of course. I promised.

"Wash up." Mother.

His father rubbed his son's head. *Why is that?* they both wondered. Because inside that skull is my son. Like petting a cat, Joseph figured.

At dinner the payment was exacted: "I want you to go back to school," his mother said.

Joseph looked at his father. His father met his eye for a moment and then found something more interesting on his fork.

But school's out, he wanted to say, only that wasn't the school she meant. She meant spaz school, school for hand language. And she knew he knew it.

"You're eleven."

Ten, you said, his father's look told her, but she ignored him.

"You can't put this off any longer. I—we—can't let you."

He shut his eyes and shook his head.

"Tell me what happened today," she said softly. "Go on. What were you thinking? What did you see? What smells will you still remember when you're old?" A noise like a cough escaped from her. "You had grease on your ear when you came home. How did it get there?" *If you were watching from the edges.* She was crying now, just the start, just a wetness in the white of her eye and a catch in her voice. "What's under that dug-up ground, and how does it feel to a barefoot boy?" *Why do you smell like beer?*

He closed his eyes again, still shaking his head, as if that would stop it.

"I'm *selfish*," she said, bawling now. "I want to know what he's *like* inside."

"Helen."

"Well, I *do!*" She closed her own eyes and put her face in her hands. "I do. And he won't learn the signs to talk to me."

I'm talking! he shouted. Look at my face, Mother. Look where my hands are, what they're doing. Look how I sit. Watch my eyebrows. I talked to you the day I was born, and I haven't shut up since.

But there was no arguing with her. He went up to bed without agreeing to anything, but knowing this future without seeing it. Its possibility would keep repeating until he found a way to stop it. He paused to look in on his sister, out of the bed with bars now for six months. She was sleeping with her bottom hoisted.

He patted it down until she was flat. Joseph didn't think anything at her; he'd only come in to watch her sleep. She had the smallest ears he'd ever seen on a human being, tucked so close to her head they looked like gills. Her hair—light brown, like his—curled over her forehead in sculpted commas. He wanted to count up the hours she had left and find how many of those she'd spend unconscious, but before he'd barely started he stopped. The unconscious hours, if they were anything like his, were as important as the others. Dreams were only a little different from real, especially if you lived somewhere in between the two.

The moon spilled in and over his bedroom window, leaving shadows. Even the soft things in his room—cap and jeans and his stuffed pony—grew corners and knife edges. In that sort of light the barriers between this world and the others grew transparent, and a clawed hand could part the fabric without effort. Even a child could push through it. He hated nights like these. He put a chair against the closet door and got headfirst into bed. Dad would come up soon.

Even in this weird, milky light, though, even scared, he fell asleep to the rumble of their voices in the floor before his father looked in on him. And when he wakes a few minutes later, he knows immediately by the size of the bed and the warm head beside his that he is in that ax-carrying future with a woman he doesn't yet know.

He tries not to move—he tries not to *breathe*—but the effort not to (or maybe the sound of his brain clicking on) awakens her, and she rolls toward him. The hairs on his thighs bristle, an ancient warning. She snuggles against his chest, and he feels for the first time that with a vision of his own future comes a body too huge for him, all its parts made for somebody else and delivered to him by some administrative mistake.

He catches one of her hands and holds it.

"Mmm."

Go back to sleep, he thinks. Willing a thing sometimes works, as it does this time.

He lies stiffly and watches the bedroom ceiling sprinkle with morning like raindrops that bounce back off the top of the dresser. The woman's blonde hair in a soft fan is indistinguishable for a moment against the white, scalloped pillowslip. He stares at a wallpaper that is almost pink, but not quite, an intricate floral pattern, looking for design. The quilt under his hands is rough or smooth in squares and diamonds. When is this? Does he have children, and does he know their lives as he knows his own, in this elliptical near terror?

She's pregnant with their first child. That knowledge soothes him for some reason, and he pulls her closer and starts to doze.

He dimly recollects seeing, on a trip to Arizona with his parents, an ocean where there wasn't one. Perhaps it's only in his imagination. And how many years in the future was it when the stars wouldn't line up right?

The quilt under his hands becomes a carpet, and in it he sees the shapes and colors in woven threads of everything that's ever lived—even a bacterium lays down a reddish-brown herringbone track—and as he rises above it like a spirit ascending, he understands its mosaic pattern: a burst, the Bang that has in its start its own destruction. He sees his own life there, a place for the thread that will be Joseph Carl Taft, not yet a color, not yet even a length. That squiggle is his family.

Does he owe his mother what she says? Yes, probably. But not now. He'll speak someday, his hands moving as if playing an invisible instrument. (He thought once that he would speak through a clarinet or a saxophone, but he hasn't the ear for that.) He will have long conversations with his mother, at the window in the light, but she'll come to that speech so late, after arthritis, that she'll slur her words with her fingers and the effort of a conversation will tire both of them.

The woman stirs, and he moves in an unthinking response to accommodate her. What did he look like at moments like this in that other time, the one he mostly lived in? Catatonic? Was his bottom in the air now, too, and was his father patting it back into place? He feels frail as a teacup.

When he awoke again, the night was moonless and he was where he should be. His room and the house with his parents and sister in it ticked like a clock. He slid into shorts and a T-shirt and went out. He stood with his spine to the screened back door and accepted like a cat the cold smells. The dark-in-dark landscape was changed, but it had nothing to do with the lack of light: he'd breathed in the smoke from those burning sycamores, had ridden on a machine that cleared the way for the bulldozers to level the land ("Catskinners," the man had called them), had watched men planting sewer pipes to not-yet-built houses. Water next, he'd been told, then storm sewers, then foundations and streets and curbs, then framers ("Still wood and brick, not those metal studs yet"), then plumbers, then electricians, then roofers, then drywallers—whatever they were—then painters, then landscapers. Then families. Plans for a golf course. Then boys on bikes and the next summer.

Joseph walked the circle of cleared property as surely and safely as if it were light. The night's not silent to a silent boy, and even under the night noises—leaves, small scurryings, distant traffic, the popping noises the earth makes as it stretches like a house—he heard a murmur from the future: the opening and shutting of doors, the flick of light switches, the snoring of neighbors in their beds, the rattle of raccoons or cats in garbage cans. His vision of the woods (woods no longer, already now) replaced with houses and streets suddenly made an impact on his heart's eyes. He won't be able to throw a rock without hitting a fence or a window or a car's fender. When he prowls these same grounds at this time of night next summer, some other person, some stranger, will be awake (he sees the blue flicker of a television from an upstairs window, sees a curtain parted), and when he's older still the cops will be called. *What's he doing skulking around my front yard at three in the morning? Doesn't he belong somewhere?*

He's in his own house, suddenly, in his parents' bedroom, leaning with the length of a teenager at their window and staring out at a black, wet-shiny street, wondering what Mrs. Alliseni is doing coming home after midnight. Where has she been? What's that noise in her cooling engine? His parents are out somewhere themselves and he's been babysitting Louis, not Louise. It's his privacy he's wanted to keep, but he can't. Like every child and beast of the field, he'll be thrust into the human community, and it will overwhelm him. *Father sold the land.*

Mrs. Alliseni closes the car door with her hip, straightens her dress with a brush of her fingers, and then tugs at herself where her thigh meets her bottom. She peers through the windows of her car one last time and goes into the house. Joseph thinks he can follow her inside if he wishes, and that's a new power, but the disembodied thought outweighs the dirty thrill and he thinks about what he knows worries his father: *my future isn't hidden from my son,* and the fact that his father's caught wanting to know it and not wanting to know it, both equally and both at the same time. He doesn't dream the worry is his daughter. Joseph, at ten-almost-eleven, hasn't seen his father's end, but he knows it now standing in their bedroom, or rather he can know it now if he wishes, and he has to hide it from himself, like not answering a phone, because it's not yet time to know. His mother's helplessness is the reverse of this. *Pick up the phone,* her look says. But she will never in her life be able to point and say that to him because he'd have to stand there stupidly and breathe into it like some obscene answerer.

He walked on into the unlit un-neighborhood, afraid of his new knowledge that nobody ever escapes the frustrations of childhood. Privacy was impossible, and control over the future, even when you knew it, was impossible, and refusing to join in with all of it—making love, buying groceries, *cutting wood*—was, well, impossible. It's daylight suddenly, and he throws his hands up and shuts his eyes to keep the sun from harming them. He spreads his fingers slowly and looks out like a baby playing peekaboo, or a cataract patient after surgery. This is forward but not far forward, and he hasn't moved from this geography. Every other lot has an ugly square gouged out. The clay sides in the holes have split and lean like icebergs. Rainwater has collected in their muddy bottoms. That one, he decides, walking to its edge, is his sister's grave.

A small leafless tree had stood just here, he's nearly certain. He'd have tied the ribbon around it if he'd known, but it's the middle of a lot, he tells himself, and the contractor or tree counter or somebody would have seen it on his plans and pulled it, and if not, then the homeowner would take it down because the pool one way or another is going to be a fact. It's none of that other stuff; it's this double, triple, braided life, like that of some UFO abductee's, that's impossible. And to prove it, night arrived again like a camera's shutter, and he stood with a numbness in his bare feet on the place that wasn't yet air, wasn't yet water, was nothing less or more than packed, hard ground.

He knelt on that spot and prayed, as he used to do when he was smaller and more scared. It was a habit he'd grown out of lately. His father had taught him how and let it go at that, but it still appealed to him, this idea of talking silently to somebody who listened.

I've got what happens to old people, don't I, but backward, I guess. It isn't a disease, is it? You've planned this. I saw the place I take up in the carpet. I'm an experiment? You've planned *this? I never fall into any of the holes that tomorrow is full of—like this one, like Louise—and I never blink and find myself going under the wheels of a truck. And it's too weird that I'd be allowed to see the future just by accident and not have a way of telling it. So you're watching, flicking the switch. But what am I supposed to do? Jump when the electricity goes on?*

Learn Sign, but that was his mother's voice, not God's. God didn't say anything. As he got up to go back home to watch Saturday morning television, he thought that maybe Time was our last prison, but the first to make the break from it needed somebody to run with.

He was sitting cross-legged at his cartoons when his mother came downstairs to make breakfast. The possibility facing him seemed to play itself out on the screen. He could stand in front of her for a few seconds to let her know it was a message, and give her a hug, and she'd say, "You'll try, then?" and he'd nod. Then she'd swell up again with crying, and so to give her back her dignity he'd go back and sit down in front of the TV and she'd hide her head in the refrigerator. His father would drive him to the school later in the day, and they'd put him in a class with the other damaged kids, the ought statistics. He'd draw the Witch, this time. The superhero he was watching on the television stopped beating on the bad guy and turned to look at him. "Mang, wass out," the cartoon said.

The TV goes out, just like that, and he's on his feet in front of it, and he knows when he turns around what he'll see.

"Look at me."

Joseph doesn't want to.

"*Child*, look at me."

The one friend he'd made at the school in one of his earlier attempts, Roger, mostly deaf but not mute, had warned him of her: "Mang, wass out. She *tough*. She"—his hands had flashed, swatting furiously at gnats—"bahks your ears. 'Course, my ears dead anyway."

Joseph had known that he'd get assigned to her sooner or later; punishments you could see always fell on you like debts.

He lowers his center of gravity like a tomcat and roots himself to the floor.

"I won't tell you again."

With other adults this was a preamble. He thinks not, with this one. He faces her.

"All right. Give me your hand."

He surrenders his left one.

She turns it over, as if she plans to read the lines in his palm. "You wash this, ever?"

He lets it go dead.

"Everyone speaks with his hands. You too. I've watched you with your parents. You're *expressive*, but you're not *specific*." She draws signs in the air too fast for him to follow and then holds her hand in a fist in front of his eyes. "That's what you'd like to say to me, if you could."

I don't want to say anything to you, he thinks, and he has a fist up too.

"Joseph?"

His mother.

The TV murmured behind him. He wanted to hug her, but that would start that future in motion, so he ran past her through the kitchen and out the back door into what had once been a backyard big enough for a boy.

What looked like moss at the bank but wasn't crawled with young mosquitoes. This was the farthest border of his father's sold property, where spongy, rust-colored ground widened into marsh and the shrubs and tall grasses on the other side climbed swiftly into willows and hickory and ash, flinty box elders, and a single pink dogwood. After that, he didn't know what; he'd never crossed because of the snakes. A tree frog blew three flute notes. Here there'd be chiggers and ticks along with the mosquitoes. Panthers, some said. Cottonmouths. 'Gators, maybe. Stupidly, he wished for shoes. A bullfrog groaned like a board being stepped on. He put his foot down on the slick, sweating side of a flat bottle and nearly slipped. He smelled the neck—whiskey —and threw it into the muck, where it landed with a smack. Fish. Herons too would stalk this place; he'd keep an eye out for those slate-colored wings. A fall of dead trees was a possible crossing, but it looked chancy. *Pre-car-i-ous.* Another tree, dead too but still standing, might go over with a push. *Widowmaker.* An owl's daylight call, like a breath blown through a cardboard tube, made him duck. Hawks. Mice. Raccoons and 'possums. He thought of that carpet he'd seen in the dream, each life linked to the other, and as if one consciousness were linked to another, too, he knew that the owl in the hickory was thinking, *boy, house, machinery*.

With the camping gear in the garage and the clothes in his room, he could live out here. He could steal the food he couldn't catch. He'd be the tall, skinny, pale freak living in the marsh, the wild man with tangled, dirty hair, a bogeyman to the children of those boys on bikes. He raised his hands in claws and tried to look frightening but gave it up immediately, feeling the future weight of that ax in his hand, reminding him of the firewood that needed splitting. The weight of future chores bent him over. What's the use of running away from home when you know what home you're running to?

The land rose in humps as he knew it would and got so thick with trees it would be hard work going on. He'd been this far before and had given up because the marsh showed no sign of ending. But that day ends and the trees divide like magic. The clear morning grows in the space of a breath into a damp afternoon as hot as murder, filling with cloud, and there's a bridge of hand-hewn planks and rails in front of him. He walks across it and through a thin stand of butternuts and chalk maples whose shadows buzz with insects and onto a golf course where three men stand over their balls in the rough and the fourth shades his eyes and looks directly at him.

"You're not thinking of going in there for it, are you, Harry? You'll get eaten."

"Somebody's coming," Harry says.

Joseph waves, acknowledging that.

"See a ball land in there?"

Joseph shakes his head.

"I'll drop one, then," but he isn't speaking to Joseph, even though he's still looking at him, wondering, Joseph knows, where he's come from.

He crosses the fairway behind the men and follows them at a distance, intending to take advantage of the future for once and walk home along an easy back azimuth that's been cleared of trees. He skirts the green as one of them pulls the flagstick, knowing he's interrupted an intimacy of some kind, and he feels their eyes on him until he's gone from sight.

Joseph has to wait to cross the next fairway and even so is nearly hit. Somebody a long way off yells at him, and he moves away. He angles toward a bench at an empty teeing place. He needs to think, but dodging missiles in a place that isn't built yet seems an unsuitable time.

He hears chatter (or rather, hears it stop) and looks up to see two white-haired women in Bermuda shorts pulling their clubs behind them on spidery carts. One nods to him warily. The other, imitating one of his aunts, opens her arms as if she's going to hug him and sings out, "Why, *hello*, there."

Joseph waves *hi* with his finger ends and wants to run, but his leg muscles lock up in the aunt-receiving defense. It's an instinct he's stuck with, like the armadillo that has no choice but to jump straight up when it's in danger, usually into the grill of a Buick. If she pats him on the head he'll blow his whistle, and then she'll have a heart attack and die.

His life makes sense; he's sure of it. He repeats that to himself like a prayer.

"Would you like to play with us? Or behind us? Or we'll wait, if you want to go on."

These are awful moments, in his own time or another. Silent children are rude or dangerous.

"He doesn't have any clubs, Millie."

"Now, why didn't I notice that?"

He hopes the other woman will tell Millie why she never notices anything, and Millie will pout or (with any luck) cry, and the first one will pretend to wait it out but will finally console her, and while all that's happening he can slip away. But the other woman ignores Millie and stares at Joseph. "Are you waiting for someone?"

He shakes his head.

"Are you supposed to be here?"

He almost nods but shakes his head again instead.

"You see there," she says to Millie, apparently settling the discussion they'd had before he'd heard them. She'd seen from a long way off that he hadn't any clubs. "Run along, then," she says. "This is a dangerous place."

You don't know the half of it, lady. He glances down at his hands to get a sense of his size. He's fourteen, maybe fifteen. And not speaking. They're scared.

Joseph gives her back her look and doesn't move. The heat settles on all of them and then pushes down on their bones like a thumb on a tack. There's no sound at all for a long moment—not even birds—and then he hears the distant *pock* of a struck ball and the spell breaks.

"Tee it up, Millie, and let's go."

The two women walk to the farthest-forward tees, take short, awkward swings, and follow their balls that skitter along the grass. The one who isn't Millie looks back over her shoulder at him one more time.

He thinks again that his life must make sense. But this isn't the place, after all, to sit and figure it out. Already he can see a foursome coming his way. Joseph spots a dark thicket between two fairways and heads for it, counting on imaginary fingers his earliest experiences of dislocation. Perhaps he can find some order in categories.

First, that ocean in Arizona, then the stars that have never fit, and finally the dozens of landmarks his parents have pointed out that he couldn't see. He has a memory, he thinks, of being carried from the car at a scenic overlook and his mother oohing at a waterfall that to him was no more than a wet trail on the rock left by a very large snail. So very early on he'd been inserted into places—and *times*—that spanned an unguessable number of years.

He steps into the thicket and there's a root waiting to be sat on, so he sits. It's twenty degrees cooler here. Second, and now he holds up for real his first and middle fingers, household accidents: dropped dishes, itinerant furniture, sticking windows, flat tires on the car. Daily warnings of dissolution on a smaller scale.

He straightens his ring finger. Louise. Come back to her.

Four: the aftermath of his life without her, like sitting here on this golf course. He folds the little finger back down so he has three, and then folds all of them into a shape he wants to strike with.

This hasn't anything funny in it anymore, as it had when the stars rocketed from their right places, or when a dish slipped from Dad's hands as he dried it, then he warned him in pantomime, then watched it all happen as it had to. His sister's coming tragedy and his glimpses of his own adulthood panicked him. He'd resisted half a hundred times writing on the notepad next to the refrigerator, *Louise will drown in a neighbor's pool*, for a dozen changing reasons: the unswerving, helpless fact of it; the miserable short life she'd have left; the miserable life they'd make for *him*; and the weird, sideways truth that it was all his fault anyway. Telling them would just push what wasn't fixable off onto people who weren't as prepared as he was and weren't much good at fixing things in the first place. Though his father has an intimation, he thinks. More than once Joseph has seen the worry scuttle like a rodent behind his gray eyes.

Maybe the household warnings were designed to make him take his sister's coming death seriously, and the geologic changes he'd seen and barely remembered (those incidents outside sidereal time) were there to make him believe the hand behind it. *All right. Now what?*

The thicket is so private, and the air so cool and still, he thinks he might get an answer this one time, but a golf ball rattles around in the limbs above his head and drops into his lap. Surely this isn't God's doing too? He hears another ball hit from the tee, and he knows with premonition instead of foresight what its flight will be, and sure enough in a second it clatters off the same limbs and drops between his crossed legs to lie with the other one.

Joseph stands up. *Why not just tell me if you don't want to talk?* The answer is returned immediately: *God speaks in events*. He peeks out. The sun is being covered by torn flags and dark ropes of cloud. It isn't until he has left the thicket and run across the fairway to the woods that border the swamp that he really understands the moment. It's the whistle on its cord swinging around and banging against his shoulder blades that reminds him.

He misses speaking now, certainly, and he'll miss it even more later on, he is sure, but at this age what he misses most is hollering. To whoop. To pour his voice into the world and mix it with the air. What does he *sound* like? That's as much us as anything, our own time-bound fingerprint that we send in front of us, over the wires, into places we'll never go. Into space.

The envy he's felt around other kids is that one. He's never sung—as he's heard other boys do when they don't know they're being watched—the nonsense syllables that give them such pleasure. *Keeoka roka oka doka roo*. Would his real voice, after the first static of disuse, be high, low, gravelly, clear? Was it destined to be sharp and irritating (as his mother's could be) or liquid and pleasant (as his mother's could be)? The sound of himself he'd made up a long time ago and kept buried, his mind's voice, was persuasive and rich and dark as coffee. *Keeoka roka oka doka roo*. He hoped when it was done percolating inside him his voice would emerge like water through sand.

He's running hard now, for the sheer pleasure of it, a boystreak across the growing-dark, green and steaming landscape, singing with his feet and pumping arms and lungs. Thunder cracks so close the slap of it catches him with both feet off the ground and suspends him in the air for a moment. The lightning buries itself in the swamp, and the mud boils. A human echo, "Fore!" carries faintly to his ringing ears, and he turns when his foot lands (feeling larger and heavier now) and looks squarely at a white ball, a zero at his forehead. And then, as if that thunderclap had carried him there, he was back in that other morning, the one he'd run to from the television, the heat and the golf course and the last remaining doubt of God's existence gone.

But lost. In a forest on the wrong side of the swamp. The lessons were getting easier, coming clearly now as if he'd found the right station finally, and this one was: don't try to run from home. *I won't*. He turned his bare feet in what he knew to be the right direction, and like a boy in a fiction—a myth, a fairy tale—he traveled the dark woods back to the house without fear.

His father knocked the first half of *shave and a haircut* and came in when Joseph answered with two raps—*two bits*—on the desk. He sat on the foot of the bed and crossed his legs at the ankles, the way his mother did. "Let's talk about school."

Here it comes.

"I know you don't want to go back there."

Joseph surprised them both by shrugging.

His father, disconcerted, hunted for words. "You've messed up my speech, Son," he finally said. "Does that mean you're willing to try, or does it mean you think we'll make you go no matter what, so why fight it?" While Joseph was thinking about just what it did mean, his father said softly, "Because we won't. Your mother and I won't force you to go back."

No?

"No." His father took his hand. "That's a promise. School was hard enough for me at your age—it is for all of us, probably—without what you have to go through too. But your mother has a point."

Joseph conceded that.

"She's not alone. I want to know what you're thinking and feeling too—desperately, sometimes—but more than that, I want you ready for the world, so you don't end up living your life as a suspect." His father was back in his prepared material now, moving smoothly.

Joseph, with his newly found intuition humming noiselessly, knew exactly what he meant, but his father explained it anyway.

"All you can do now, really—with people outside this house, at least—is answer questions with yes, no, maybe."

That was true.

"Is it not a fact that you had an appointment with the deceased on the night in question, April twenty-ninth, and that the aforementioned meeting was to be held at midnight, by the river, in the junkyard?"

Joseph smiled. Colonel Mustard in the conservatory with a candlestick.

"Aha. Should we or shouldn't we take that to mean that you didn't not meet with him?" His father stood and spread his arms. "Young Mr. Taft has proved by his own admission, ladies and gentlemen, that he was the last person to see him alive."

Joseph grinned, waved his hands, and made the air shimmer.

"Oh? The last person to see *her* alive?" His father grinned back. "I was just telling your mother that you're older than we think." He sat and let the smile fall too. "But let's keep this to ourselves for a while, okay?"

Sure, Dad.

"This can be serious."

Joseph knew. He remembered the look on the woman's face at the golf course, four or five years from now.

"We'll learn Sign right along with you."

Joseph crossed his heart.

"I promise. And we'll do it here at the house, not at that place. We checked; we can get someone to come in."

Who? Joseph wanted to ask, but he knew who.

"We'll sit around the table after dinner, before Monopoly or Hearts."

His father was still selling the program, which reminded Joseph he hadn't nodded yet. He hugged him instead, which left his father, as always, both happy and a little bit afraid.

The teacher from the school came the next night after dinner, as promised. His parents were doing dishes when the bell rang. They looked at each other and then at him, so Joseph got up to answer the door. The teacher, of course, was the Witch.

"Hello, Joseph." In her mouth, in his imagination, it was an old threat finally realized: *I told you I'd see you again, little boy*.

He asked her in with a small, stiff bow.

She put her purse—as large as a typewriter—on the table and shook Frank's and Helen's hurriedly dried hands. Then she shook hands with Joseph. (He'd almost held out to her his left one.)

"I guess I'm about the only teacher at the school that you haven't had," she said. "But I've heard about you."

And I've heard about you.

"They say he disappears sometimes," she said to his parents by way of explanation.

"Disappears?"

"Goes blank. For quite a while. They didn't tell you?"

"I guess we should talk about that," his mother said.

"Let's leave that to its own time," his father said, receiving simultaneous grateful, quizzical, and uncertain looks. "How about a cup of coffee for now?"

"Cream and a little sugar."

She means Yes, please, Joseph wanted to say. *This is going to be* hard.

Frank had the same thought and hesitated over the coffee pot with the cup still upside down in his hand.

"The sugar's in the cupboard over the stove," Helen said, misreading him.

"Milk will do, I suppose, if it's all you have," the Witch said.

Who's got cream anymore? Frank wondered. "It's two-percent," he said.

Way to go, Dad.

"Oh. Well. As long as it isn't that blue, watery substance they shouldn't be allowed to call milk, I can—"

"We'll be sure to have cream tomorrow night," his mother promised.

"—make do. I don't want to be a bother."

Frank and his son exchanged glances that skidded and locked in midair.

When she'd taken the coffee and two-percent and sugar and a spoon to stir it with and a saucer to hold under it, she said, "First I'll pass out some materials"—she dipped a shoulder toward her purse, as her long fingers were busily curled around the china—"that will explain how I work: a list of *dos* and *don'ts*, if you will, and checklists—"

A checklist?

"A checklist?" his father asked.

"Yes, Mr. Taft—"

"Frank."

"And Helen," his mother added, and nearly pointed to herself.

"A checklist that must be filled out each evening before our session together. And a different one, after. One for each of you."

"Should we put our names on this checklist?" his mother asked. "What's on it?"

"Well, after I finish—"

"Has he brushed his teeth, washed his hands, things like that?"

"No. Well, yes, there are some *hygienic* questions—" She said *hygienic* as if the word itself needed cleaning.

"You mean, Is he free of lice? Things like that?" his father asked.

Whoo-hoo!

The Witch made a face and leaned forward, carefully unwrapping her hands from the cup like tissue from a present, and putting the cup and saucer on the coffee table (the first time it had ever been used for coffee that Joseph could remember) just as slowly stood and smoothed her skirt. "I'm beginning to see," she said, "why the child has had so much difficulty at school."

"The *child*—" his mother said.

"So do I," his father said.

"The education of a child requires a threefold concentration: the child's, of course, the teacher's, and the parents'. If we can return—"

"The *child*," his mother said, "bathes regularly. He is well mannered. He says *please* and *thank you,* although you have to be on the lookout for it, he does it in his own way, and he operates in all other respects like a normal eleven-year-old, without any sort of—" She looked to her husband for help. "Any sort of—"

"Difficulty?" Her smile could chill champagne. "Can he articulate what is important to him?"

"Preflight instructions," his mother decided, though it still wasn't what she wanted. "He's not a test subject."

"Thank you, Mrs. Taft; I am aware of what he is."

"*Who* he is! And thank you for coming, whoever *you* are."

The Witch raised an eyebrow.

My mom can take you, Joseph thought.

"Miss Elena Woolcroft. They didn't tell you?"

"They told us," Frank said.

You didn't. My parents are funny that way.

"Perhaps I'll leave the materials in any case." She ironed another unseen wrinkle from her skirt. "After you look them over and give this more thought, you might decide differently."

She unpacked her purse in a quiet that would have warned off ghosts, leaving an impossibly square stack of printed forms next to her coffee cup. "Well, then, good-bye."

"Good-bye."

And that was that. Her car went down the drive.

"Did you notice," his father asked when the sound of it was gone, "how, when she put the cup back on the table, the spoon in the saucer didn't clank? How did she do that?"

"She probably needs nerves of steel in her work," his mother said. "Perhaps—"

"Don't start, Helen. In ten minutes it'll all be our fault."

"But—"

"Do you want *the child* to study with her?"

"No." She whispered it. She shook her head. She mouthed the word *No*.

"We'll find another way." He turned to Joseph. "You're not off the hook."

Joseph, on tiptoes, kissed his mother, squeezing the tops of her shoulders in a hug, and then his father, full on the lips, and went up to bed. They could have seen in the lightness of his step, if they'd needed to, that he was whistling.

In the morning his mother had waffled and his father was wavering. Joseph saw in their tiredness that his mother had talked until her husband was nearly beaten. He knew how she'd done it too: she'd replayed the scene in their dark bedroom, taking in turn each speaking role (because his father wouldn't play), analyzing each speech, every inflection, parsing the sentences, and, with that special talent mothers had, each eye- and finger-twitch.

"We were a little harsh to your teacher last night," she said to her son over breakfast.

Your teacher.

Joseph shook his head vigorously.

"Yes, we were. We got our hackles up over bad manners and then showed her worse ones."

His father sighed tiredly. This was a script he'd heard a dozen times by now, Joseph was sure.

Help, Dad.

"I think we should call and apologize. What do you think?"

Joseph hated it when she forced him into compliance with a decision she'd already made, a tyrant telling the peasants they could vote.

Joseph shook his head until it hurt and then got up (a little dizzily) and retrieved the forms from the coffee table.

"Yes, let's look at those," his father said, taking them. "We did agree to read that checklist before making any decisions." He skimmed the first page with a finger and then turned to the second. "Here's one: *Are hands clean and manicured?*" He looked at his own finger and then held it up and waggled it. "I wouldn't pass."

"She won't be holding *your* hand, Frank."

"Oh? I thought the class was for all of us." Joseph heard the tone and measured pacing in *for all of us*, and was heartened. His father always rose to his son's defense along certain carefully considered battle lines, and one of them was not making children do something parents wouldn't. "And here," he said, turning another page, "is a series of skills-building exercises. We all have to do this too, apparently."

"What skills?"

"Dexterity. Finger exercises, like your hand doing little pushups. And attentiveness. We've got to practice our paying-attention skills, Helen. Here's a diagram"—he held it up so she could see—"of good posture."

"Oh, for goodness' sake."

Joseph wasn't sure if her exasperation was directed at his father or was once again turned in the direction that deserved it, but he thought it a good time to leave them alone to work it out. His father was rereading the first page now, and smiling. He slipped away from the table without either of them noticing, and that, he knew, would speak for him more than eloquently.

The back door beckoned, and he was tempted, but he went upstairs to see his sister.

Mother had already fed and dressed her and taken her out of the crib. She sat in the exact center of her small room, surrounded on all sides, as if with pillows, by large, soft animals. She put her arms up when he came in.

Hi, Sis.

She wanted his whistle. He put it behind his neck and sat down and held the braided lanyard out for her to play with, which was enough this time. She tugged on it fiercely, making him bob, and giggled delightedly. Louise had a good handful of words already, but she never spoke when they were alone.

He looked around idly at her stuffed toys, recognizing among the new ones those he had given up to her: a bear (not a teddy), a dog (it used to bark, or at least grunt when it was squeezed), a whale (its wide blue flukes and fins a satiny material). At her age he'd lain on that for hours and sucked his thumb, but it wasn't one of her favorites. He remembered guiltily how he'd fought to hang on to the pony—had hidden it, in fact—and how he displayed it prominently in his room now because he felt he had to, although it no longer fit there. He'd be willing to give it to Louise if she wanted it, but she didn't, and he'd made such a fuss he was stuck with it at too old an age.

Joseph rearranged the pile over her small protests and then lay down next to her. She kept a hand on his whistle cord. He pulled the whale close and put his cheek against the satin. He'd ridden its back, lying on it while watching *Captains Courageous*—

The door opened. "How's my sweetie do—Oh, hello, dear."

He waved at his mother.

"Mom," Louise said, a statement of fact, not need. Joseph always thought of her as Mother; he wondered why.

"I thought I'd take Louise into town with me. Would you like to go too?"

He shook his head.

"Dad's gone to work, and I have groceries to get."

So the other thing is still undecided, he thought, but she surprised him.

"We're back to square one. We'll figure something out later. I shouldn't leave you here alone. . . ."

He circled his head with a finger.

"I know you'll be good."

He put his hands together.

"All right. Stay away from the machinery."

He nodded reluctantly.

"I mean it, Joseph. Or you'll come with us."

He nodded more firmly, and crossed himself.

"Got to find another sign for that," she said under her breath. "Your breakfast is still on the table. Come on, little girl—*un-huh*, you're heavy."

He stayed in the room after they'd left—even after the car had gone—trying to recover the beginnings of an idea that hadn't even come with a picture. Something about watching television had sparked it.

It wasn't until that evening, lying on the floor watching his sister and the television, that he got one of the pieces back, and he went upstairs to Louise's room and brought down the whale.

"What do you want that for?"

He gave his father a slowly exaggerated shrug and a puzzled, inward stare, which meant he really didn't know.

Helen gave her husband a look that said, *Maybe he's more upset than we thought.*

Frank gave his wife a look that said, *Maybe so.*

Joseph saw both his parents' looks, read their semaphore accurately, but didn't correct them. He hoisted Louise out of the soft-netted playpen and laid her belly-down on the whale, and he took her small hands in his and windmilled her arms until she kicked her feet in delight and was making, his parents saw, swimming motions.

In a dream he hears Mother saying, "Don't go," and sees his father pointing directions to places he's never been and doesn't know himself how to get to. In the dream Joseph says, "Good-bye," hearing his own voice as he's always imagined it. Waking, he knew it had nothing to do with his parents and everything with his sister: that in it he was his mother and his father and it was Louise who'd said good-bye.

Sifting the meanings from dreams had always been as easy as seeing through glass, so the truth of his reasoning was inarguable. Which made it that much sadder; she'd be leaving soon.

This, the third summer since he'd escaped the Witch, was the last summer his sister had. Even though his parents had signed her up for the YMCA swim class before she was two and she'd leaped from her brother's arms into the water the first time like a homecoming, and even though she swam in every pool in the neighborhood in all weather and stayed under so long she must have gills, the picture of the future never changed: Louise died in Mrs. Alliseni's pool next month.

It was still dark, but he unrolled himself from his limp sheets and braced himself at the windowsill to stare across the street at that hateful house. An orange streetlight showed him that his hands were growing into the size and shape of the teenager he'd visited so often. Everything, he thought, staring at the fine hairs on the backs of his fingers, was coming true. A better brother would have invented ways to make his sister terrified of water.

He rummaged through a heap of flannel shirts on the closet floor, pulled a joint from the pocket of one, slid the window up an inch, sat, and lit it.

You are *a punk.*

Joseph had thought his father was going to hit him when he'd flipped his mother off, and when he hadn't, he'd flipped him off too. Banished to his room, he'd torn the screen door in his violent hurry to get outside. Forbidden to come back, he'd holed up in his room. Mother sneaked him food. *What use is talking when nobody means what he says? What good is there in seeing what happens if it all happens anyway?*

He pushed the window farther up and flicked the roach out onto the wet lawn. Where Dad will find it. *How have you become their tormentor?*

Fourteen is an angry age. The rebellion of testosterone in the blood materialized in his classmates as it couldn't in him: in sullen silences like a palpable odor. But nobody could do it better than Joseph, having been born to it. Adults couldn't even *ask* him questions, unless they wanted to fight him to get the answer on the board in chalk, or in laborious finger pictures. The other kids took their lessons from him, and—except for a couple of the girls—the classroom became a quiet, seething place. The school—the normal one—sent him home finally. They had to. They sent him home more than once. That had been the beginning. He'd added the up-under-the-eye-brows glare when he got back from his first suspension, and then a couple of tough-guy fights, and drugs and cigarettes and beer. Only posturing, but in no time at all he was the nightmare that keeps all teachers awake.

Dad's wrong; you're not a punk. You're worse.

The stupidity, he thought, almost raising a hand to bang his forehead, was that he wanted to learn. This other attitude was a role that had been placed upon him, and he didn't know how to release it. He was mad at everybody now: Mother, Dad, Louise, himself, the kids at school, his teachers, God.

Him most of all. Joseph's grown convinced that if he'd only stayed on that golf course a year from now three years ago, the ball heading for him, if not killing him, would have given him back his speech (he thought of it lately as something that had been taken from him, instead of not given), as happened sometimes in newspaper stories he read. A blind man struck by lightning not only wakes up and sees for the first time; he sees colors no one else knows. Why had God aimed the cure at him and then pulled him out of the way?

He saw humpy rooflines growing against a slightly less dark sky. He wished now that his grandfather hadn't had any money when the land was put up for sale the first time, and that his father hadn't needed any when it was sold the second time. And he wished for what must be the umpteenth time that the Allisenis hadn't put in a pool they never used.

A kitchen light went on in the Parker house. He drove dump trucks for a living and got up early, even on weekends when he didn't have to. His son, Lonnie, and Joseph were friends, maybe, or will be again, perhaps, when school starts in a couple of weeks. He wasn't sure what *friends* meant. He couldn't tell anymore, but he suspected that for the rest of his life in school he'd have only followers.

Joseph slipped a rubber band from his wrist, where he kept several, and knotted his hair in it, and stared again at the Allisenis' house. Lights wouldn't go on there for a long time yet, though the bug zapper by their pool lit the underside of a tree an eerie blue.

He knew every part of that backyard, from the dozens of pool-hopping neighborhood parties, but mostly from the visions of his sister's death he never stopped receiving. He'd seen that from every angle. He didn't need to close his eyes to see the wide, warm sandstone walk curving around the kidney-shaped pool and leading to the back porch, or the tile mosaic around the pool's edge, the 2′, 4′, 6′ marks in primary colors. Red, yellow, blue. The Allisenis' backyard was the showcase of the neighborhood. And now, as her death grew closer, he was getting visions of the services and the burial as well. He'd seen a scorpion-shaped backhoe digging the deep oblong where they'd put her, and his own hands on a shovel handle sweeping the dirt back in. His parents and neighbors stood around like rocks on a carpet of Astroturf while a black stranger reaffirmed how unfair it all was. When he finally got the vision (if it ever came) of the headstone and the date on it, he'd kidnap her—steal Dad's car—and drive her someplace safe.

He put on jeans and a shirt and went down the hall to her room. Louise lay at attention on top of the covers: on her back, her feet together, her hands at her sides. Even in that lack of light he could see the sheen of her open eyes. A thrill of fear tickled his groin.

Joseph was attempting to sort out how all those visions of drowning could be wrong, or whether he was living another part of this horrible future's aftermath (but why would they lay the body out on the bed?) when she raised a hand and said, "Hey."

She scooted over to make room because sometimes he liked to sit with her and hear what dreams she'd had (though not as often lately), but he stood in the doorway and didn't even wave back. An engine started up outside: Mr. Parker in his pickup on his way to work. *Don't steal the car.* He blew a kiss she couldn't see in the dark and ran downstairs to catch him.

Parker's heart nearly stopped when Joseph's shape loomed in front of his windshield, but then he recognized the boy and rolled down his window.

"Morning, son. Something wrong?"

Joseph shook his head. He tapped his chest and the hood of the truck.

"Sure, come along. But you need shoes."

Joseph held a finger up: Wait.

"Hurry, then." *You couldn't get Lonnie up this early, not even with the promise of machinery. Not even with dynamite. The Taft kid, though, never seemed to sleep.*

Joseph sprang onto the passenger side of the truck's bench seat holding workboots and socks, and Parker only just managed to save his coffee.

"Got enough room there?"

Joseph nodded.

"Move what you need to. The plans can go up on the dash. I think you're sitting on a box wrench."

He'd taken the boy to work with him before, and usually the kid was a pleasure to have around—eager, helpful (and quiet, of course)—but he had seen the change in him the first part of this summer. Lonnie had too, he guessed. It seemed the two were friends, then good friends, then hardly friends, by turns. Parker couldn't keep up with it.

At the equipment yard on the site he watched approvingly as Joseph climbed up on the bumper to lift the

Diamond Reo's hood and pull the oil stick, jumped down and ran a hand over the inside tires looking for nails, then stuck his head under the rear end to find anything in the drive train that might be leaking.

Parker sipped his coffee and threw the kid the keys. "Fire it up." That grin was why he'd brought him. It occurred to Parker—and not for the first time—that construction was a place a long-haired kid with an attitude who couldn't speak might make a living. It was too damned noisy, most of the time, to talk anyway. He thought sometimes that everybody ought to carry a whistle.

When the engine was warm, it was light enough to see. Parker raised a thumb. Joseph waved back through the window, and then the dump body lifted slowly, about halfway, before the kid brought it down again.

Parker rapped on the glass. "You didn't pull the tailgate pins first. Got a boulder or something in there, you bang it all to hell. Or a raccoon crawls over the top and we bury it without meaning to."

The kid nodded *Sorry*.

"S'okay. It's empty. You know you only had it up halfway?"

Joseph shook his head that he didn't.

"Looks different from the cab. Looks like you're going to tip over. All right. Take it around the yard once and fuel it up and we'll go. And put your hard hat on."

The day's work was easy, as it was all on site on mostly level dirt, and after Joseph had the layout straight, Parker let him drive. Another new housing development with its requisite golf course. How many of these things could the country stand? Seemed he'd done a dozen of them.

Joseph cradled the steering wheel with the insides of both forearms, his hands loosely locked at the top the way he'd seen Parker's. Take the dirt out of there and put it over here. D8 Cats cut it down, loaders heap it into the truck, D6s spread it out when it gets where it's going. It amazed him, still, to see how quickly men changed landscapes. He thought it a shame that trees couldn't be picked up and moved and set back down (nearly everything else could be); instead, a tree without a protective ribbon got killed and a new one planted. Hills got leveled, low spots filled, level spots raised, and the birds and turtles and rabbits and gophers and snakes that survived had to do the best they could somewhere else. It wasn't right.

But even so, Joseph liked this work, almost as much as he liked riding around on the big yellow, earth-moving machinery, and he liked the way Parker found a way to get him paid in cash somehow. Not always, and not a lot, but often enough that he felt he was doing more than taking up space. He liked it well enough to consider trying to get work with Parker when he was done for good with school, so Joseph changed his mind about stealing the truck at the end of the day, trailed by cops and sirens, and taking the consequences; he'd steal it at night instead, and try to get away with it.

He knew the keys on Parker's ring he'd need—padlock on the equipment yard, ignition, padlock on the gas pump—and Parker had so many he wouldn't miss them until the next day. He put the two padlock keys in his pocket at lunch and slipped the ignition and door keys off the ring just before he handed it back at four-thirty. He checked the pickup's odometer as they left the yard and again when they got home. Eight miles; a two-hour walk if he didn't dawdle.

"See you again tomorrow?"

A nod. *Almost a certainty,* Joseph thought, especially if he wanted to slip the keys back onto the ring and get out of this crime after. He fingered the twenty-dollar bill Parker had given him and wished he'd left it on the seat in the pickup's clutter.

After dinner he went out to case the block, even though he could have done it sitting in a dark closet. He'd be okay until he started driving over people's lawns, and then things would happen in a hurry. He mapped it all out in his head: come in from that direction and go up on the curb here, stop in front of the azalea, then straight back into the fence. Fifteen feet more to the edge. Haul ass and hope Parker takes his time putting on a bathrobe and shoes. Nobody else matters.

He went up to bed early but couldn't sleep. When he was sure the others were, he slipped out and walked the long way to the job site.

It all unfolded smoothly, naturally, like a flower opening, and he guessed that seeing the future before it happened had given him a skill—either picturing events or responding to them or something even more mysterious: being in sync with them somehow—that was useful. He might do well to choose a career (like this one) where that would come in handy. He unlocked the chain-link fence and left the gate open, then started the truck and checked its fuel gauge. He wouldn't need the key to the pump. The only part of the plan he hadn't been able to work out completely—and he'd thought about it all day and all the way here—was how to get dirt in the dump truck. He hoped somebody had gotten lazy because the machinery was always kept behind fences at night.

Everybody but Parker, apparently, had gotten lazy. He found keys in toolboxes, under seats, behind visors, and dangling from ignition switches. Perhaps all the operators, moving to some barely heard command, had for the first time in their working lives not taken their keys home with them. *So pick one.*

He chose a backhoe like the one he'd seen digging his sister's grave. Although it was a long reach for its bucket over the truck's sideboards, its small engine and rubber wheels would make the least noise. He drove the dumptruck out to the nearest spoil pile and then walked back, started the backhoe, and drove it to meet the truck. The backhoe was as easy to operate as it looked; it had to be, as every rental shop in town let civilians have them for the weekend. It steered like a car, with accelerator and brake, and the bucket and its controlling arms moved on a joystick. Any kid who'd ever played video games needed five minutes of practice; any kid who'd spent a part of the last three summers watching men work needed none at all.

He worked in the dark, afraid that lights and noise would bring the curious, and he'd already done what he could about the noise. The first bucketload, more rocks than dirt, sounded like explosives going in. He tried to hurry and at the same time crouch in the seat prepared to flee. It was better after that. He imagined the truck settling on its springs, and he tried to fill it level, but that was much harder than he'd thought. *This machine's too short.* When he had it half loaded he could see even in the dark that the truck was listing. *That's more than enough, probably.* He returned the backhoe to the yard and buttoned up, then drove Parker's Diamond Reo onto the road and turned on its headlights.

Joseph had only shifted from first to second on the job site, and from neutral into reverse, had never driven the truck on the roads and hadn't wanted to, and now they looked scary. Worse, the truck leaned so badly he had to sit at an angle just to see straight. *Weight'll pop the tires if you don't watch out.* He left it in second all the way home, although its straining engine sounded enormous at two o'clock in the morning. Half a mile from the house he found the nerve to lift a hand from the wheel and turn the radio on: an oldies station, but he couldn't bring himself to loosen his grip a second time to tune it. The other stations, anyway, were country.

His street, his house, his dad's car. The Allisenis'. All dark, all asleep. All according to plan. All right. *Unless she's already drinking this early into his future and came home right about now. No, her car's in the driveway too.*

He jumped the curb, riding the clutch, and didn't get it stopped quite in time. The azalea went under the bumper. He ground the gears trying to find reverse, panicked, revved the engine, and ground it again. *Gonna snap the teeth off.* He let it idle in neutral, took three deep breaths, and inched the gearshift with his fingertips into reverse. It slipped in as silently as Parker did it when he shifted, showing off, without the pedal.

The house and fence grew in his mirrors in the glow of his backup lights, and then the fence went under his rear wheels with a thump and a shriek that sounded human. He stood on the clutch, hit the Power Take Off, and pulled the lever to raise the bed. *Good-bye to the prettiest goddamn pool in the neighborhood.*

He was still leaning sideways to counteract the truck's lean, and his clutch foot slipped. A hundred thousand dollars' worth of Diamond Reo, his neighbor's livelihood, rolled toward the pool. Even as he put all his weight on the brake and clutch, Joseph realized he'd made a worse mistake: the tailgate pins. The bed was all the way up. He felt the load shift and knew it couldn't get out. The rear wheels slid in, pulling the truck up on its end so it was for a moment vertical, Joseph staring through the windshield at the stars like an astronaut, and then, gouging a scar in the pool's tiled bottom, it capsized like a torpedoed battleship in a shallow harbor.

"I think the place for him is jail."

I don't like you either, Mrs. Alliseni.

It could be another party except for the fire trucks, police cars, the ambulance, that dump truck and five cubic yards of topsoil in the pool. Certainly everybody else was there. His father stared at Joseph as if he didn't know him. His mother looked away. Parker's eyes kept shifting from him to his drowned truck and back again. The headlights, eerily, still glowed under all that mud.

"The boy's soaked," one of the cops said. One of the ambulance people handed him a towel.

He'd had to roll the window *up* to get it down, to get out. That had thrown him. You'd think an upside-down truck would be the same place as a right-side-up truck, only opposite, but it was worse, a place he'd never imagined and had figured out how to negotiate barely in time. His last bubbles were going up with the cab's when he finally managed it. He hadn't the breath left to blow his whistle when he surfaced. And he couldn't see because of all that dirt and diesel fuel. He'd wiped the mud from his face and seen the whole neighborhood watching. *The wild man in the marsh.*

"Need someone here who signs," the same cop said. "You're his parents, right?"

His father nodded. "We don't sign," he said. "But neither does the boy."

"How do you *talk?*"

Well, we don't, much, do we, Dad?

"Child neglect," the medic said. A murmur moved through the crowd, the kind that makes the rounds just before they hang the horse thief in a bad Western.

Joseph stood up, shivering, and put his hands out. *Cuff me.*

"Let's get him away from here, anyway, Lou."

"You live where?"

His mother pointed across the street, but it wasn't much better in his own living room. She pulled the drapes, but the neighborhood was lit now, everybody milling, and it would have felt eerie even without the strobe lights from the emergency vehicles and the radio static from the police cars.

"You stole the truck," one of the officers said.

"Maybe I'd better call a lawyer," his father said.

"Where were you on April twenty-ninth?" Geez, Dad, how'd you know?

Joseph shook his head at his father, nodded at the police.

"And you lost control of it in front of your house?"

"Yes." Dad.

Joseph shook his head again.

"That's all," his father said to Joseph. "I'm going to insist on the lawyer."

"We can't talk to him here, we're going to arrest him."

"Then arrest him. Don't say anything, Son."

Joseph grinned at that, as scared and tired as he was, and his dad, after a minute, grinned back. Everything would be all right; Louise was safe now.

"The boy dumped a truck"—the policeman, Lou, worked those words over silently for a minute, knowing there was something wrong with them, and then went on—"in your neighbor's pool. I think we ought to get this straightened out right here, right now."

"Can't get it straightened out right now," his father said. "Can't get it straightened out until I call a lawyer. *Then* you can get it straightened out. Nobody's hurt. Everybody's upset, but nobody's hurt. Take him with you if you have to, but if you leave him here I can guarantee he's not going anywhere except up to bed."

That *up to bed* is a nice touch, Dad. Remind 'em I'm just a kid. A sociopath perhaps, a truck-stealing, pool-wrecking lunatic maybe, but a kid. Joseph coughed. He would have sneezed if he had known how to fake one.

The cops and his father argued quietly, back and forth. He started to fall asleep.

"I don't know. Call the sergeant."

"You joking? He's on his way over. Be here now, but something's kept him."

"Kid ought to get dry at least."

And so Mother took that opportunity to take him upstairs. He was dried off and put to bed, but there wasn't a lot of love in her touch.

A lawyer, the next week. A pair of social workers. His parents, when the house was cleared of strangers, impersonating the lawyer and the social workers. Spaz school on the horizon bearing down on him like a train, and he knew what the engine looked like.

Louise had somehow slept through the fuss and didn't understand any of it. His parents wouldn't explain it to her, so he'd sat on the curb the next morning and pointed at the Diamond Reo when it was raised by two gigantic tow trucks, winched dripping from the water like a muddy whale, and then pointed to himself and made steering motions, but he didn't think she understood that either. She cried, but only because she'd lost a pool to swim in.

The cops filed the complaint they had to, and the lawyer his father hired told them they'd be in court in a month. The Allisenis were threatening a lawsuit, even though his father had agreed to fix the pool. Parker refused to join the Allisenis or even show up in court when the time came. In fact, he knocked on the door a couple of evenings later looking embarrassed.

"Insurance'll cover the truck," he'd said, waving away the possibility of further financial ruin for the Tafts. "I'd like to talk to Joseph, though."

"I'll bet. I wish he could talk back," his father said. "We'll make out all right. We always have."

Frank gave Parker an appraising look. "Don't kill him; he's the only son I've got. Anything else is okay."

"Maybe just a walk around the block."

Parker was still in his work clothes, and when they got outside he shoved his hands into his jeans pockets and stared at the house across the street.

"Quite a mess."

Joseph stuck his hands in his pockets too.

"Thought we got along fine."

Joseph nodded.

"It wasn't an accident, was it?"

No.

"You've got something against the Allisenis."

Yes. No. He made swimming motions.

That took him a minute. "Something against their pool?"

Yes.

"Well, at least you didn't burn the place. It's fire I'm afraid of, myself. In a neighborhood with the houses this close together, I picture the flames leaping from roof to roof. A careless smoker a block away burning me out. But geez, kid."

Some *neighbor* harming me. Joseph hung his head.

"I'd like to know, son, why you did it. Like I told your folks, insurance'll cover a new truck and the rental on the one I'm using in the meantime. But you and I, we were friends, weren't we?"

Joseph nodded.

"I've got a set of rules for myself, and for my family: be honest, work hard, help people in trouble, things like that. Nothing earthshaking. You've upset all that for me. If you'll just tell me why, I won't tell anyone else."

Joseph kept his head down, thinking about how to do it.

"Will you? Please?"

He nodded.

After a wait, Parker said, "You want to write it down?"

Joseph shook his head, then lifted it. He could say all he needed to with the sign language construction people used. He pointed to his eye.

"Look? See?"

A finger on the nose. Charades. He threw his arms open.

"That's a puzzler. Everything? You see everything?" Parker frowned. "Like God?"

Yes. No. Yes. Each of them deliberate, measured. Joseph reached for Parker's wrist and Parker jumped, so he tapped his own wrist instead.

Parker looked down at his watch. "This?"

Yes.

"Not see, then. Watch?"

No.

"See *and* watch."

No. He tapped his wrist again and spun a finger.

"Time?"

Yes.

"See time. You see time?"

Yes. Joseph pointed forward.

The understanding was in Parker's eyes; the acceptance was not. Finally, hesitantly, he said, "You see forward in time? You see the *future?*"

On the nose.

Parker took a step back. Who could blame him? "I've got that right?"

Yes.

"Your parents know you think this?"

Yes.

"I'm going to check that with them."

A shrug.

They went back into the house. Parker took his hands out of his pockets and didn't know where to put them. He pulled his work gloves out of his back pocket and held them. He cleared his throat twice. "Your son tells me he can see into the future," Parker said. He raised his eyebrows. He smiled sheepishly.

Mother and Dad exchanged a long, tired look.

"How about a cup of coffee, Mr. Parker?" his father asked.

"Did you hear what I said?"

"Maybe you'd rather have a drink?"

"Only if you're going to tell me it's true." He laughed. It sounded nervous to Joseph.

"I've got scotch, I think some vodka, maybe some gin—"

"Jesus," Parker said. He sat down in Frank's chair. "Give me a beer, then."

"Sorry. I don't have that."

I've got some in my room.

"Anything. Bourbon, scotch, I don't care. You think it's true?"

Frank nodded once. "Joseph's not a vandal, Mr. Parker, not a danger to anyone. He's not a criminal, I don't think. He did what he did for a reason he won't tell us. But I trust that he had one."

He made a couple of bourbon-and-waters and handed one over. "I guess it's the same with us not learning to sign. We should have, I know. It only makes sense to do it—hell, I think we're facing a neglect charge because we haven't. The good Lord knows I've fought with the school district long enough, and I've only won temporarily because medically they can't prove he's a mute. But with a boy like him"—he pointed, needlessly—"knowing what he knows—and I *know* that he knows—you let him go his own way more than you would another."

Helen sat beside her husband and took his hand. Frank squeezed it and said, "In other words, Mr. Parker, I trust him."

"I always have too," Parker said slowly. "But this isn't possible. Is it?"

"I can't convince you of it, and I honestly don't want to try. But this might help: there's nothing wrong with his voice box."

"You mean he could talk if he wanted to?"

"It's not a matter of wanting to," Helen said. "It's not that. It's the—what?"

"Wiring," Frank supplied.

"Okay, the wiring is different. Up here."

"Of course, it's *us* he's driving crazy." Frank smiled at his son, who didn't smile back. "It'll all make sense one day."

Parker downed his drink and stood up. "Hell."

"I don't think there's any religion in this, either way," his mother said.

Joseph nodded in agreement.

The date for the adjudicatory hearing had been set for three weeks and a couple of days, and was almost here.

"They'll charge him every way they can," the lawyer had said, nearly a month ago now. "Being in possession of a stolen vehicle—several, in fact—breaking and entering, criminal mischief, reckless endangerment, destruction of property. They should have done a tox screen and didn't, so my guess is you'll be saved a couple of charges they would have had otherwise."

Well, that was true.

"What do you suggest?"

"Get him a nice suit, shined shoes, a haircut. Teach him to smile. Take his whistle away from him." The lawyer had picked up his briefcase and walked to the door. "Then, when I give the signal, have him kiss the judge's shoes." He'd tried to smile. "It won't be so bad. Lots of community service, maybe one of those boot-camp environments out in the woods. He won't get jail time."

Jail time jail time jail time.

"Find a way, if you can, to have him explain it all to the judge. That'll help the most."

This evening, the night before the hearing, Joseph was still trying to put it all into words. He sat in his briefs in the living room at the coffee table with a tablet and two chewed pencils. He'd hammer on the table once every half hour or so in his inarticulate frustration and ball up another sheet and throw it at the fake fireplace.

His parents chose to ignore it. "I wonder where she's got this new idea of hers, swimming naked. Everybody's got to fight to keep clothes on her."

Joseph looked up, but it wasn't a message meant for him, as he'd thought it was, wasn't a reproof for sitting in the living room in his underwear.

"From that new friend she's made, I would think," his mother said. "Louise is over there right now. I like them, but I don't know about their children, Frank."

Over where? Joseph asked with his eyebrows. *What people? Whose children?*

"The Searses," she said in answer to her son's question. "They moved in six months ago, remember? Next to Margaret Beasely. You've seen them at parties, but maybe you don't remember them because they always leave their girls at home. Their pool was finished last week, so your sister introduced herself. She sniffs them out, you know. It's shaped just like the one across the street that you—" She folded her hands in her lap. "It even has the same pretty sandstone paving around the edges. They hired the same pool architect, the same landscaper. And it's a good thing, seeing that—"

Joseph tipped the coffee table over, scattering ice cubes and Coke, leaving a plastic cup spinning on his undone and undoable speech to the judge, and ran as he was, half naked, out the door.

He raced across the Allisenis' yard, and some part of him registered an unnamed emotion when his feet sank into the wheel ruts still in the lawn. Grass was easier, but on concrete he'd have traction, so he swerved back into the road and turned the corner leaning like a motorcyclist, his ponytail flying.

His feet slapped down painfully with every step, not because of the concrete (he had feet like hooves this late in the summer) but because his muscles were tied to his heart. He slammed into the slatted fence. It sagged, sprang back. Superman, superhero. *Man, watch out*. He hammered on it, kicked it with both callused feet, felt his little toe snapping.

Joseph burst through the splintered gate just ahead of the Searses running out their back door at the commotion, and he caught like an afterimage one of their daughters standing in the lit living room behind them because it's she who will want the wood. He has now in both skinned hands a skein of kindling. He runs, as they do, braking at the pool's edge, and the three, four (and then five) of them meet at opposite sides just in time to see at the bottom her naked trunk, her feet like roots, her arms waving.

She'd always felt that only children are capable of everything

Gabriel García Márquez,
Chronicle of a Death Foretold

Spirals of green ribbon dangle from newel posts and creep like ivy across windowsills and pew backs. White roses humming with bees spill over the altar rails. Their petals, like blown leaves, speckle the red carpet. Paper daffodils and tulips are taped to every vertical surface. Children not yet born will cut them out from stiff construction paper in Sunday School. The guests clutch in their laps fistfuls of baby's breath tied with ribbon. She wants spring in autumn, and Joseph smiles at that. His father, in the first row, grins back, thinking the smile is meant for him.

The bride's side of the church is nearly full, the groom's side almost empty. He stretches, pulling against the dark suit jacket that tugs across his back, and stares at a big, bald man he knows from somewhere, somewhen, who seems to be gleaming, as if he has carried into the church with him his own illumination, and at Parker, who winks. Louis, in a suit too—or, anyway, the replica of one—lies sprawled half on, half off, his mother's lap. He stares back, bored. *So that's my baby brother.*

A woman behind him is hammering on the organ's keys, an instrument too loud for this small place. She leaps, midphrase, into "The Wedding March," and the hairs on Joseph's arms stand. Side by side up the narrow aisle his bride and her crippled father lean against one another so close that Joseph's thin shadow crosses both of them. Stained light throws colored squares on her blonde hair and ignites tiny fires along the seams of her beaded gown. Her father rests for a moment on his strong foot, gives his crutch away, then topples into the first pew next to his pretty wife, who holds his cane. That, Joseph thinks, looking from mother to daughter, is a future every wedding guest can see.

She *is* beautiful. He inches her closer, careful of all that gown around her heels, staring with nothing short of wonder at his luck. A tiny stud in a shape he can't make out glimmers in her ear. The braided lanyard around her neck is as comforting to him as, apparently, it is to her. At her décolletage, where her netted breasts hide under satin, a pin glitters, a tiny bow. Behind her ivory veil his bride's eyes shine with tears.

He tries unobtrusively to wipe the sweat from his palms onto his trouser legs. This is love, he trusts; *I just haven't gone through it yet.* He should be the one in white. He reaches for her gloved hand and took his mother's, spotted with rain, at the gravesite. Dark earth spoil on either side lay piled higher than the coffin.

His muscles lost their hard, bunched energy, and his heels, in that roller-coaster feeling he's well used to, sank an inch into the newly turned dirt. He flexed his cramping fingers. His parents and neighbors (Parker and his son, Lonnie, both in jeans, taking a stolen hour from work; the whole Sears family, girls, dressed in the same new shade of dark blue) and both pairs of grandparents stood on squares of Astroturf that were heaved like poorly laid bricks, but he'd walked forward, apparently, to say good-bye. His mother wanted him back. Joseph slipped free of her grip, carrying out a motion he didn't remember starting, and, kneeling, curled his hands through one of the coffin's shiny handles. It had subtle ridges on the undersides for gripping. *I'm sorry.*

It was so still he could hear the quiet *tock* of raindrops on the rose wreaths, white too, on the calla lilies, on the black papery silk sashes—*In Memory*—that wrapped them, on his father's mirrored black wingtip shoes, and scalp. They beaded and ran on the coffin, worked under the collar of his shirt, filled the hole.

This teenaged boy on his knees seemed the parent. The minister, The Rev Roy he called himself, stepped around the coffin and the waiting grave and knelt beside Joseph. He put his hand over the hand on the handle. His was badly scarred, and the bones in it made a tent behind the knuckles.

His lips to Joseph's ear, he said, "She's in the palm of Almighty God."

Joseph shook his head. She's in the carpet.

"She's with the family we belong to forever." He meant the species, us, *Homo Deus*, the ones with souls.

Joseph gets a picture of a kind he's been seeing more of lately, as vivid as the others but without the steel of truth: at a dinner party, a dark, hairy hand next to his on the tablecloth reaches for a butter knife, wants the butter. Passing it, he wonders, *Do we share a language? What does that squat figure who sucked the marrow from an antelope's bones have to say to me, a boy who lives in pictures he'll have to spend his whole life sorting out? And how will he do it? But maybe language began that way; maybe I'm relearning an old one.*

The scene is nearly as real as the Allisenis' pool—the Searses' pool, the copy, he reminds himself—but as that hand's extinct, it's clearly impossible. What does it mean?

Look at the face.

He sends the thought to his muscles, but halfheartedly; he can't bring himself to turn his head and do it—he knows he'll recognize in it his mother's eyes or his father's nose or his own chin.

"Son?"

Joseph understood he had to let them get on with the service, that Louise couldn't be kept here any longer. *Perhaps that's her next to you.* He understood he had a life of his own to finish and, if that time in bed were true, at least one more to start. But he couldn't make his knees work, couldn't raise himself from the wet ground.

The Rev Roy leaned closer still, his rough cheeks against the fine blond hairs of Joseph's face. His skin was so black it shone purple at the bridge of his nose and the pouches under his eyes. His breath was warm and smelled of milk. "The congregation's getting soaked, son. Come stand up front with me and we'll sing her on her way." The minister's ugly hand tightened, gently, on the boy's.

Joseph tried to look away from it but couldn't.

"A horse stepped on it," The Rev Roy said. "My father rebuilt it in his workshop. Hammer and tongs; Ahab and the carpenter. Do you know that story?"

Joseph didn't.

"I'll tell it to you another time. It fits with mine. Ahab's story fits with everybody's." He wiggled his fingers and then leaned back and put one to his lips. "That's a secret," he said, still quietly but loudly enough for the others to hear.

As if Joseph could ever tell secrets.

"Come on, now." He lifted that horrible hand from Joseph's and offered it to the boy.

Joseph exposed his throat, smooth like a girl's, without an Adam's apple.

"Doesn't matter," The Rev Roy said, his voice booming suddenly. "Sing with your heart's voice. That's all God hears anyway." He raised Joseph by the shoulders of his new suit and, gathering him in a hug, walked him to the narrow end of the hole, on the crumbling edge of the precipice. "Look down there into it, son."

It looked a lot deeper than the six feet Joseph thought it should be.

"None of us escape this." He spoke to the family now, to the guests, and Joseph realized he had been doing so for some time. "I'll bury some more of you before I'm done, and before you're done, some of you will bury me. There is no knowing on this side the whys and wherefores. Not very often does He let any of us understand the plan."

But I've seen it. I've been lifted above it to see it all.

The Rev Roy cocked his head, as if he'd heard. "He seems a cruel God, doesn't He? Seems uncaring of innocents. Seems content to let fire and plague and flood and our own animal natures destroy us. Seems unreachable, sometimes, in our furious prayers. Seems"—he paused—"cold as space." He tipped Joseph forward until he was cantilevered over the grave, held by that broken hand. He whispered, "That's a doorway, son." He pulled him back from it. "Make sure you go to Him before He comes to you."

Joseph, just fourteen, had already been places the minister hadn't and knew God to be exactly as cold as space, and maybe even colder than that. He knew too that The Rev Roy was preaching to the choir: nobody (including Joseph) had ever for a moment thought Louise's death was *God's* fault. He saw satisfaction in at least one wet white face as the minister manhandled him to the edge of the grave and then held him over it, rubbing the puppy's nose in his mistake. A larger coffin, not his sister's, is being lowered there. *His father.* Joseph twisted free, stumbling over the berm of new dirt, skidding on the Astroturf until his new shoes bit, and then he ran, dodging headstones and shedding clothes like words. *The wild man.*

He could do it. He could live in the swamp the developers had been forced by law to leave along one side of the houses because it was a sanctuary for birds and turtles and alligators. His father hadn't had to sell all of it after all, shouldn't have sold it, and wanted it back now. But his mother said she wouldn't take one step down any road that led back to a courtroom. "And we'll take cash in this family instead of liability any day of the week."

"We've got enough money, Helen."

"And enough trouble. There's college to think of."

"What if Joseph would rather have the land than the education?"

"Too bad," she'd told Frank just a week ago. "He's going to college. And after him, Louise."

But not Louise. And Joseph wouldn't go to college either. He wasn't even certain he would finish high school. At that age he sees himself working for Parker, driving another, newer Diamond Reo. Louis might go, might give Mother what she wants, but he wasn't here yet and, from the one look he'd had at him in church, wasn't formed yet in other ways, might not ever be formed inside correctly, and promised his parents nothing except perhaps a life of crime. *Like me.*

"You can't force that boy, Helen. He's got his own mind."

"Then make him use it, Frank."

"He'd rather use his hands."

Joseph, having crept halfway downstairs, had seen his mother clearly. She was facing his father. She turned in a complete circle, checking for who knew what, and when she was facing him again, she said, "He can't use both?"

"I didn't have to give it all up."

"You didn't know. But now that it's gone, think, Frank: kids all over the place, barefoot like Joseph, falling into holes, stepping on snakes, doing God knows what to themselves. We don't need the lawsuits, honey. We don't need anything more."

She'd never imagined a threat in the other direction, inside the suburb, nor imagined one aimed at her younger child. Joseph had been the one in danger, hadn't he? What must she be thinking now?

By the time he reached the paved paths that served as roads he was naked except for his light-blue briefs and a shoe on the left foot he couldn't get unknotted. He wondered why all the species on God's earth needed to hide from their own kind, but that thought hadn't even formed itself until after he'd shucked his underwear, was behind the wheel of the hearse, and had the car going. The big door in back shut itself.

He'd never driven anything but a dump truck. He reached for the gearshift the car didn't have, and his hand hit the windshield. Against the glass he saw it was trembling, so he put it in his lap, where the shock of his own flesh made it fly to the steering wheel without his willing it.

How far do you really expect to get like this? he wondered. How long before the cops notice a naked fourteen-year-old tooling around in a stolen meat wagon? They'd light up their roof, give the siren a twist, and he'd pull over. Wouldn't he?

"Where's your driver's license? Whoa. Never mind that, boy, where's your *clothes?*"

Strewn on a wet, grassy slope downhill from Louise's grave. It's okay, though, officer, my sister would never have recognized me anyway.

He missed a turn he thought was probably his and accelerated to run a yellow-gone-red instead of standing on brakes he wasn't certain of. Slew this big car around in an intersection and kill somebody. The newspapers would have some fun with that. Running red lights, though, ought to accomplish the same thing. Where the hell was he? Weird that he could grow up in a town and not know where the cemetery was, how far it was from his house, at which compass point.

He bet all the other kids knew. Bet they dared each other to go into it at night. Bet with their one-day-at-a-time lives they had everything plotted, certain, known: this far from here to there; take this much time by foot, by bike, by car. Joseph saw their arrogance at school, in the classroom and on the playground, and knew it was their lack of knowledge that made them mean. This was how everybody else in the world survived their uncertainty. *So what's your own excuse?*

Three more turns and the hearse was in town, stopped at a light near the theater. He knew his way from here. He turned right when he should, and there was one of the kids he'd been thinking about, Bobby Spizac, riding his bike on the sidewalk where he shouldn't, making people move out of his way. Joseph pulled up next to him, waited until the kid looked, waited until he saw that he was naked, and then gave him the finger. Then he drove the rest of the way home.

The tremor in his hand had crawled all the way up his arm now. He was sitting on his bed watching it as if it were hooked up to wires and a battery when he heard his parents pull up. He got up to look.

"Here we go again; we've raised a car thief, Frank," he imagined Mother saying, trying to skirt but still stumbling against the bumper that had more chrome than her whole car, coming up the walk with his balled clothes in her hands. But he saw that her hands were holding only each other—she'd left his clothes where he'd dropped them—

and the tears that streaked her makeup had nothing to do with him. She shouldn't have to see that hearse ever again, and never in her driveway. He heard her slow step on the stairs, heard her bedroom door close softly, and waited for his father to follow her up and knock.

But he came in without knocking and closed the door behind him. He leaned against it in case his son bolted. "Put some clothes on," his dad said.

Joseph raised his hands to his throat and choked himself. When his father only stared, Joseph lifted the pillow from behind him and put it over his face.

"I don't care if you feel suffocated; put some clothes on. You're too old now to be naked. Besides, you're shaking."

Joseph dropped the pillow to his lap but didn't move to dress.

"It's too much for your mother right now," his father said. "It's almost too much for me. If it's too much for you too, I'm—we're—all—lost."

Is it too much, Dad? I almost got married today. I almost buried my sister. I stole another car. It's easy as one, two, three. Mother has a broken heart that I haven't seen far enough into the future yet to know if she recovers from. He wanted to raise a hand, both hands, but couldn't think how to form a gesture that could carry all the cargo. *I've had a full day, Dad, in the last couple of hours. These sorts of things should have some time between them, don't you think?*

But none of that showed on his face. He stared back at his father with what he knew to be glazed, unintelligent eyes. *How do we do that so easily? Turn the light off inside even while we're thinking?* While he'd had the chance, he should have followed that butter knife and hairy hand up an arm to the skull, afraid or not, just to see what lights if any had been winking there. His other hand, now, was trembling too.

"Mind if I sit down?" Frank was in midair, sitting without waiting for a response he didn't think he'd get, when Joseph too has nothing under him but air, is weightless for a moment with a headache that has made him blind.

He feels grass spikes under his shoulder blades before he goes numb. A voice he doesn't recognize says, "You all right, son?" Another says, "Check to see if you killed him. My God, it looked like you caught him square in the forehead. And it was a good drive; I'll bet you lost forty yards."

That golf ball from another time that he'd seen coming once. Then he's out completely; everything's black, even the voice, and he's living unconscious in his own future.

What the hell's the point in that? he thinks when he wakes, as if that last knowledge had been formed and then left blinking like a telephone message. Sharp corners of adhesive tape tickle his eyelashes where the bandage on his forehead is nailed down over the bridge of his nose.

He sits up, rustling like a snake in a polka-dot paper gown that's tight across his chest, but it's his father in bed and Joseph sitting next to him, a mirror image of the real moment back in his room after the funeral, the tightness not on his chest but in it, and The Rev Roy has his good hand resting on Joseph's shoulder.

His father's hair has thinned. His face is a motley of primary colors: at a diagonal, one side is more blue than pink, the other more yellow than blue. Joseph looks to The Rev Roy for an explanation, but he must have already been given one because he only gets another shoulder squeeze.

The Rev Roy's hair has gone marvelously white in the intervening years. It reinforces Joseph's feeling of dislocation, of negatives. They stand there together a little longer, and then The Rev Roy says, "It's times like these we realize what complicated clocks we are."

You don't know anything, Joseph thinks.

"All those tiny gears and springs," he says. He holds up a thumb and forefinger as if gripping one of the parts. A pancreas, Joseph thinks for some reason. Maybe they'd studied it in school lately, next month ten or twenty years ago. "But he's out of danger now."

Is he? None of us is for long.

Proof of that, as ever, is swift. In another room, painted a softer tint of that same hospital green and furnished like a bedroom, he stares between a woman's legs—his wife's, he hopes, but all the views he's had of her so far have been tantalizingly indistinct, as he wishes this one were—and she's blowing, huffing, whistling, sweating, groaning. She levers herself up on her elbows to catch his eye. Her mouth forms the words *Help me*, but a surgical team is there, so he slips, not unwillingly, back into darkness.

Stop is the word in his head, waiting as before, when he comes to. But there's no stopping this terrifying ride. His mouth mimics his future wife's: *Help me.*

It's happened; I've lost my mind.

An outdoor television screen the size of a shopping mall is flicking through still images several dozen a second, the mirrored winter sky behind it lit with its reflections like water under fireworks. He knows this isn't true either, but true-like, a way of compressing something larger than truth, packaging it for him, picturing it. The fact that it isn't the future but futureness, that he won't have to actually live in it, relaxes him, and he slows his breathing with an effort and watches. He finds he can distinguish one thing from another in all the colored blur, that his mind can race at almost the same speed and can almost catch up, and that part of his head is busy sorting the afterimages and making sense of them without his asking.

The television turns to blocks—to small mountains—of hand-hewn stone, pocked with craters the size of his fists, oddly shaped, never square, but fitted together with such skillful precision and careful design that he can't slip the blade of his pocketknife between them. They glint in the sun as if made from metal. Weeds sprout, grow into vines, harden into roots, and climb the near vertical faces, but even with the help of centuries they can't pry the stones apart.

Through the root foliage of branches like a peepul tree's the pictures keep coming, brighter, dimmer, flashing in code, in what he finally figures out is rhythm, is song: oceans' and seas' and rivers' hidden currents eddy and swirl in lighter colors like dye, then stop, crystallize, freeze in snowflake petals with the pastel tints that ice gives water; the air hums with airplanes that look and sound like insects; the ground between is level, rock hard, wasted.

Little wars in hot, dry places speed across the screen, two or three a minute, but they seem much longer. Crop failures follow water shortages that follow floods that follow famines. Cattle are dying, heaped like those dead trees still stacked in his memory, like tires at a dump, but white with the leaching of death like sheets and towels and underclothes waiting to be washed, like the bones of dinosaurs that with enough time find mud to settle into and the patience to turn to stone. People are dying in heaps of their own. He hears a word not invented yet: *quanchron*. *We'll need it,* he thinks; *it's the measure of a lifetime of a species.*

Pass the butter. It's being passed to him. *But I don't want it.*

Hundreds of men and women—of all ages, all races, but in the same suit and tie, in the same face—keep talking, talking, talking. Joseph can see through them, to their chairs, as if they are ghosts. Behind them, U.S. Marines slink through Times Square in three-man teams, running doubled, low, under the assault of civilians.

A computer simulation of the globe spins while some huge, ungainly machine he hopes is not in scale orbits it. A camera anchored out in space zooms in until the planet has shrunk to his small part of the world, the border between the Carolinas, and then red arrows appear and point, flashing, to the town, the block, the house where he lives.

A satellite is falling. Joseph looks up into the night sky, still unable to recognize the constellations but picking out among those stranger stars a glint, a wink, a growing trail of fire that's aimed at him. *God's put gasoline in a bottle.*

The screen darkens, then lights again, one tiny light bulb at a time, and he sees that each flash is a flashbulb, each image a self-portrait of its photographer, all of whom—young or old, dark or light, man or woman, human or not—share a family resemblance, and then he pulls back and sees that the different images are only pixels in a larger picture, like one of the anniversary covers of *Life,* and the portrait made of all of them together is his own silent, serious expression.

The television was talking the news in that pale-green hospital room when he awoke, and he felt the way one does when trying to answer a telephone or a doorbell in a dream and wakes to find it ringing. His father sat in a chair at the foot of the bed reading the paper.

Jesus, I'm tired. When is this? What's this tube in my arm? He wore the paper gown he remembered, but not the bandage. *So I'll return.*

His father noticed his son touching his forehead, got up, and put the paper down. "You all right, Son?"

Joseph shrugged. He doubted it.

"You had a seizure of some sort." Frank laid the back of his hand against Joseph's face, the way Helen did when one of the children was sick. *One of the children.* "Do you remember?"

Joseph shook his head.

"In your bedroom, after . . . the funeral."

Tears started in Joseph's eyes. He knuckled them away and nodded.

"That was yesterday. Mother was here too, last night and this morning, but I sent her home to get some rest or she'll be next. I should have taken her to a motel, though; the house is full of neighbors."

You're talking to yourself, Dad. *He probably hasn't had any sleep.*

"The doctor said he'll be by again after lunch—anytime now." Frank looked at his watch. "Everybody's a bit perplexed."

Me too.

"Tell me what you can, if there's anything to tell, and I can help make it go quicker with the quacker."

Joseph smiled at that. He laid his hands together in prayer and held them to his cheek.

"Like sleeping?"

Joseph fluttered his eyelashes.

"Dreaming?"

It was a good thing, Joseph thought for the billionth time, that his father was good at this game.

"He's going to want you to write down answers to his questions."

This didn't take even a headshake, just a dead look: No. We've been over this ground before.

Now his father shrugged. "We must be the worst parents in the world," he said.

Joseph saw the sudden recognition in his eyes, Louise's drowning, and then all the weight he carried of his dead or troubled children. His father stood like a man in uniform and cried silently. Joseph held his arms out, the IV tube restraining him, and that's when the doctor paid his visit.

I know you.

"Better, yes?" He nodded without waiting for an answer. "Better, obviously."

He carried two thick manila folders bound with red rubber bands, and he dropped these on the bed with enough force to make Joseph jump. "Don't take out what

I've just put in." He grasped Joseph's wrist and forced it down, then, as long as he had it, held on to it with two fingers and counted. "Good heart," he said. "Steady. Slow. Strong. Now, what's the matter with your brain, eh?"

Frank bent at the waist, unlocking the puzzle piece that had kept him rigid. "He has a good mind," Frank said, echoing what he'd told his wife.

You've got to believe that, don't you, Dad?

The doctor didn't even turn to look. "Probably so," he said. "I don't know what I should about the mind. The brain, well, I don't know much about that either, I'm afraid, but I can read pictures." He pointed vaguely at the files he'd brought that lay on the bed. "The pictures are—what shall we call them?—interesting."

Pictures?

The doctor was pretty good at the game too. "We took some snapshots of you," he said. "Got some good ones back. Wife at the beach. Backyard barbeque. Eiffel Tower." He tried to smile but wasn't any good at it. Joseph felt better about that; the other doctors who'd tried and failed to diagnose him had been too friendly. "My name's Higgerby, son, and you've finally fallen into my hands."

The large man at his wedding, Joseph realized. Higgerby, Piggery, is what the kids at school would have called him. Being large and round and pink, he couldn't have avoided it. He might have been as miserable as Joseph, growing up.

"Pictures?" his father asked, uncharacteristically a step behind.

He's exhausted.

"Brain scans," Higgerby agreed. "Colored blobs, but colored blobs the likes of which I haven't seen before." He finally turned to Joseph's father. "Why don't you close the door and have a seat, Mr. Taft? Where's your wife?"

"Home, sleeping."

"Ah, yes. I'm sorry." He stood for a moment, looking at his unpolished shoes, trying, Joseph guessed, to decide whether he should say anything more. But what he said was, "Broca," and pointed to the left side of his own skull. "Here." He tapped the curve of his forehead. His head was large and bald and pink enough to be a medical-school model.

Broken. I knew it.

"It's the part of the brain that controls speech." He stared at Joseph. "And in the boy here, it's lit up like Independence Day. Now, why is that, if he can't talk?"

He stared so long at Joseph that Joseph shrugged.

"And I understand rightly, don't I, that he won't write? Not for conversation, I mean? Doesn't carry around a notebook and scribble what he wants to say?"

"His mother's tried a hundred times."

More than that.

"A thousand times."

"Why is that, Mr. Taft?"

"He wants his privacy, I suppose. Wants to turn what he's got into an advantage. How many kids are there who don't have to answer their parents?"

"What I meant was, why does your wife keep trying to get him to write? I had a talk with some of the doctors who've seen him, and they admit he's always able to make himself understood. Answers their questions, and so on."

"He's got a gift for that," his father agreed.

"More than you know, I think. Let me try something." Higgerby turned to Joseph. "Pick a number between one and ten." He swiveled back to the father. "What is it, Mr. Taft?"

Frank looked at his own hands and guessed. "Five."

"What's the answer, Joseph?"

Joseph held up a hand with its fingers spread. It began to tremble, but this time he knew why.

"That part of the brain's involved with that too," Higgerby said. "Nobody knows why yet."

His father took it in for a minute, then sighed and stood up.

He's not all that surprised.

Frank patted the chair. "Your turn to sit down, Doctor. Please." When Higgerby, smiling, had done so, Frank said, "We've grown convinced that he also sees the future."

Higgerby squinted at Frank and then at Joseph, pursed his lips, and pulled a small notebook from his pocket. "Give me some examples?" he asked.

Another doctor would have kept him in the hospital for days, but Higgerby hadn't even tried. "Not a damned lab rat," he'd said. "But I'd like to come visit. Is that okay? Saturdays, maybe, or Sundays'd be even better. I could teach you how to throw a knuckler, and maybe you can teach me how to fish. Do you know how?"

"They leap up into his hands," his father had said, "gasping out their lives in joy."

Let me talk, Dad, Joseph thought, and Higgerby said, "Now, why doesn't that surprise me?" and then he patted Joseph's arm and shook his father's hand and left the room before Joseph could think up the signs for politely saying no.

But it wasn't the weekend when he got home, and his first visitor (not counting the neighbors, all of whom wanted another look at the sideshow that had come their way again) wasn't Dr. Higgerby but the mortician, Mr. Small. He sat delicately on the edge of the most uncomfortable chair in the house, with his hands completely at rest in his lap. "I'd rather not see this family in any more difficulty just now," he said to Mr. Taft.

"Thank you."

"Grief expresses itself in myriad ways."

His father nodded.

"But I understand the boy has stolen other cars before mine."

"A dump truck," his father corrected. "And a backhoe, I guess. No cars that I know of." Mr. Small didn't smile. He wouldn't, Joseph thought. "He has a taste for the exotic," Frank ended lamely.

"And for whom was he grieving then?" Mr. Small asked.

"He's not a common thief, Mr. Small. There was, in fact, an emergency then too."

Joseph thought his father had stressed *common.*

"Yes. Well. I've filed a report with the police—my insurance requires it, you understand—but I'd rather not press the charges. Out of respect." Impossibly, sitting, he bowed.

"Thank you again." Frank stood and offered his hand.

Mr. Small didn't move. "But actions have their consequences, nonetheless, wouldn't you agree?"

Uh-oh.

"What do you have in mind?"

"That he should come down and wash the hearse, vacuum its insides, polish its wheels, and so on. Justice requires it."

"All right."

"Every Saturday for six months."

"That's too severe," Frank said.

Tell him, Dad.

"I don't believe it is."

"He'll give you a month, four Saturdays, and he won't wash everything in your lot, just that one. He'll do a very good job and then he'll come home, and then we'll be done with it."

Mr. Small stared at Frank for a full minute and then said, "Very well," and got up and left.

"I'd forgotten all about the car," Frank said. "They must have come by and picked it up while we were at the hospital."

I left the keys in it, Dad.

"And the man's right, Son: there're consequences to stealing."

Joseph nodded.

"Try not to do it anymore, okay?" He grinned. "A couple of years more and you'll have your license." *Then I suppose you'll steal ours.* He almost reached out to touch his son, but didn't.

The two of them made do as bachelors, cooking and cleaning up after themselves, until his mother, after three days of invisibility, came down to breakfast. She smiled almost shyly at her husband and son. Her face had lost weight, which made her eyes and lips look larger, and she'd washed and braided her light hair and coiled it on top of her head like a pastry. Joseph saw gray in it for the first time. She was pregnant already with Louis and didn't know.

I could tell her. Will it make her happy? He decided that it wouldn't, that she'd only have a month or two more to give herself completely to the loss of Louise before she found out, and that she needed that time.

What did he need? He looked at the clock in the kitchen as if it had the answer, and it did: he had to wash that champagne-colored hearse. He took his bike, leaving his dad to explain. *I should have taken the car,* he thought as he coasted down the driveway.

In town he got lost again. *Where is this place?* He tried to picture how they'd gone—less than a week ago? a year?—but all he remembered was how the other cars had flicked on their headlights out of respect for his sister. He'd turned around in the back seat and watched the taillights go out again when they were past. *Why lights?* he wondered. *Because,* the answer came, *like flowers, they're momentary; it's the grass they grow on top of you that's perennial.* He braked for a woman coming out of the dress shop, then got off and wheeled his bike through a sudden congestion of mothers and small children. The sidewalk was more dangerous than these quick streets.

He had to look it up in the phone book, but once he had the street he could find it.

Mr. Small didn't even say good-morning. He was in his office off the foyer, making pigeon sounds over the phone, what he probably thought of as consolation to another grieving parent or child. He pointed to the garage at the back of the house, its double doors open, and when Joseph walked out there he found the hearse, the hose, the vacuum, the glass cleaner, the soap, the bucket, the rags. He set to work.

He had the car wet and was soaping the hood when Mr. Small came out.

"And how is the young Mr. Taft this morning?"

Joseph looked up, nodded, and bent back to his soaping.

"Cat have your tongue?"

Joseph took a swipe or two more and straightened all the way. *He doesn't know.* He used his mother's gesture—or maybe she'd taken it from him, he couldn't remember—of holding his hand in a bud to his mouth and then opening the fingers while shaking his head, an Italian-looking provocation, he suddenly realized.

Mr. Small took it that way. "You're working off a crime against me, young man. There are harsher penalties, if you'd rather."

Mother had made him carry a card that said *I'M MUTE!* but he'd felt like an idiot, or a beggar, and had lost it enough times that she'd eventually given up. He wished he had it now. For the first time he even liked that exclamation point. *Up yours.* He thought for a second and, rather than make the effort, pulled his whistle from under his shirt and blew it at the man. *The only words I have, mister.*

Mr. Small still didn't get it. Red-faced, he squared off in the driveway as if getting ready to fight. His weight shifted onto his toes and Joseph thought for sure he was going to put his dukes up.

Jesus, now what do I do?

But he didn't have to do anything because Dr. Higgerby drove in, parking an inch from Mr. Small's backside. "How are you doing, son?" he asked before he was all the way out of the car. So it wasn't his imagination; Higgerby had seen it too. "You know the boy's mute, don't you?" he asked Small.

"Mute?"

"Can't speak."

"I know the meaning of the word. I'm appalled is all."

"At what?"

"That his father didn't tell me."

"The boy seems to get by," Higgerby said, "with most people."

"And who might you be?"

"His physician. Higgerby. We have an appointment this morning."

"He's working off a debt."

"We'll have our appointment here, then."

Small nodded and turned to go, but Higgerby said to his back, "You weren't going to strike him, were you?" which turned him around again.

"How can you ask such a thing?"

"I've seen boxers work," Higgerby said, "and I'm guessing you've boxed."

Small considered his answer. "A long time ago."

"That's enough for me. The debt—whatever it is—is paid. Let's go, Joseph."

Joseph wanted to, but saw himself run from the funeral. He shook his head. *I must do this.*

Mr. Small almost smiled before he turned again and went back inside.

Higgerby watched until he'd shut the door behind him. "You have this problem often?" At the boy's look, he said, "I wouldn't think so. But you stay away from strangers too, don't you?"

Sure.

"Lonely?"

Oh, Christ, if you knew. He ducked and rubbed the hood harder.

Higgerby didn't wait. "When I was your age, I sure wanted some friends. Other kids didn't like me, but you've already guessed that."

Joseph's head bobbed with the stroke.

"You're going to take all the gold off that hearse."

Joseph agreed, rinsed the hood with the garden hose, and moved around to soap the wide, curtained windows.

"Everybody's different, somehow," Higgerby said. "In fact, everybody's so different, nobody is, if you follow me."

Joseph kept his back to him.

"What happens when you try to talk?" Higgerby asked.

Joseph hesitated, seeing his face in reflection; then he swiped the rag across the picture of himself and moved around to the big back door. Lots of chrome here.

With Higgerby's other patients—kids too, some of them—the doctor could outlast them, get them to talk by staying silent, but Joseph threw that off, threw him off, and made him hurry. "I've brought some cards with me," Higgerby said, pulling them from a pocket, not pressing on the other front. "Just playing cards, a Bicycle deck. If I hold the back up to you and look at one, will you tell me what you see?"

This thing I've got doesn't work that way. Here was a future he didn't want, hadn't seen, didn't have to live through. *You said yourself I'm not a lab animal.* He shook his head.

Higgerby saw his mistake and regretted it. "I'm sorry. I really came out here just to talk to you, and offer my friendship. I should have stopped there."

Joseph dismissed the apology with a wave. Don't worry about it.

Higgerby walked back to his car and stood, undecided, at its open door. Joseph was invisible now on the far side of the hearse. Higgerby got in, buckled up, and started the engine; then like magic Joseph was standing at the windshield looking in. He opened his mouth in an O, a parody of horror, and out came a strangled, squeaky yawp.

When he'd finished brushing the seats and sucking up the limp petals and curling leaves from the upholstery with the vacuum, he was sweating. He closed the five doors and stood back from the car, knowing he'd done a good job. Mr. Small was at his office window watching, and Joseph guessed he didn't blame him. Without looking that way, he got on his bike and rode home.

Mother and Dad weren't there. They'd left a note on the refrigerator saying they'd gone for a walk, and it was just as well; he couldn't bear to be around her just now but hadn't realized that until she'd reappeared that morning. He'd failed her horribly in every way possible and didn't know what to do about it.

He knew less what to do about anything than he ever had. His brain was changing—this curse had never panicked him so—and so of course he'd chased away the only man who might ever help him understand it.

Joseph pulled his whistle out and shook it. His only voice for as long as he could remember, now all it brought to mind was his sister's hand reaching for the shiny bauble and her joy in gripping its braided cord. A storm welled in him, blowing through his throat and eyes, unstoppable any longer, and his parents, before they opened the front door, heard a caterwaul punctuated with whistle blasts bouncing from all the mirrors in the house.

He wouldn't be consoled: when Helen harvested him into her arms the screech intensified (they hadn't thought that possible); when Frank reached for an arm, a shoulder, his head, Joseph ducked and flailed and ran, knocking over lamps and chairs and end tables until he was upstairs in his room cornered at the open window. Still he howled. His terrified parents waited at the open door, afraid to go forward or back.

The Allisenis came to their door, and then the police came.

Frank took his time answering their knock. "It's grief," he told them. "We've had a death, his sister." And then he gently shut it in their faces as they touched their caps. They got back into the squad car but didn't go away.

The stalemate lasted another twenty minutes before Joseph's voice shut off like a needle lifted from a record, and he collapsed, still crying, in his customary silence. He heard the cops go. He heard a door close. He heard his parents cross the room like spies. He heard their arms around him, the three around each other, and he heard his sister in the water telling him that the carpet was more beautiful than he knew.

"Shh," he heard, like steam escaping. "Ssshhh."

Mother.

Heat was in her hands. They stroked his neck and arms, over and over, petting the cat that was her boy, and the heat was of the kind that builds between fur and flesh, jumping with electricity, with a charge like the air in a thunderstorm, and a rumble of a human purr was building in his chest.

"Shh, honey."

Joseph slept without dreams of any sort for what felt like a long time, and when he woke he was on the bed, but she still held him, still stroked him with fingers that left their warm trails in his skin.

He heard his father's voice outside the window saying, "How very kind, I'll give them to him when he wakes."

He yawned and the fingers stopped. A clock in him was ticking at a normal pace, and he knew that his life, compressed like Morse code, was slowed, was manageable once again.

He opened his eyes and found the whistle, hot to the touch, clenched in his palm. He offered it to his mother, but she didn't want it, or didn't understand, and with both her hands curled it again into his and pressed it closed.

"Are you hungry?"

Yes.

"What would you like?"

In that cramped, wonderful, almost painful position, cuddled awkwardly against the curve of her body, it was hard to hold his arms out in the gesture that meant *Everything*, but she knew it or guessed, and reluctantly pulled away from him and said, "I'll make all your favorites."

How beautiful his mother was. He didn't have to wonder how his father had fallen in love; he had only to wonder how the two of them—Joseph and his dad—had gotten so lucky. Her hair had come loose from the braid and stood up around her head wildly with the static charge (because her son *was* a lightning rod), and her eyes had lights behind them that played across the blues in her pupils. In that moment he would have been able to point and say, *That's what life is.*

"Take a long shower," she said, "and come down when you're ready."

A shower *was* what he wanted. *How does she know such things?* He stood under water the hottest he could make it, but his skin was hotter still and the steam that filled the room was from the fire that still filled him, from his heart.

"These are for you," his father said when he came downstairs. "One of the Sears girls brought them over while you were sleeping."

He'd have thought that more flowers would be the last thing ever to gladden him, that he could live the rest of his life without wanting to see or smell another one, but he would have been wrong. Nobody had put them in water; they wouldn't fit in water and were meant not to live. They lay on the coffee table just inside the front door in a fan on lavender tissue paper: red tea roses and pale day lilies and bluebells and sprigs of white pine and delicate dogwood like a sunrise and perfumed shapes underneath that mass that he didn't know. It must have taken a wagon to cart all of them over. *A piece of everything in the Searses' yard,* he thought. *All that's missing is the kindling I made from their fence.*

He raised his eyebrows at his father. Who?

"The oldest one, the one your age. Helen?"

"Luce," his mother said from the kitchen. "The oldest girl is Luce."

She heard me howling. This is how it begins. I thank her for the flowers or I don't. I keep them or throw them away. I hold her hand or pull her hair. Either way, we'll be married at the end of a courtship that's just now started.

He sat down to dinner feeling the wonder of events that even in real time never ceased to astonish.

Joseph had called at the Sears house the next day, nearly five years ago, with flowers of his own from the shady places in the swamp that she had never seen, and they were holding hands before they'd walked a block together, and by the week's end he'd given her his whistle, his voice (it might as well have been one of his organs), which she'd placed around her neck outside her blouse as if it were a diamond.

His mother had done this: given him love enough to give back.

That was the problem now. Luce sat in the pickup bed on a blanket he'd dragged from behind the seat, her spine as straight as the helve of a shovel, the soles of her bare feet pressed together. The zipper of her shorts was undone, and the buttons of her shirt, and even though he couldn't see her face clearly in the last moon—the left-handed one—that was up, he knew the tops of her cheekbones were burning.

"Now," she said, for probably the fifteenth time.

He ached with a frustration that went deeper than his pants. His father, all those years ago, had said he'd need one day to make himself understood clearly in court, but it was courtship where words were wanted. Who'd have thought it?

"Now."

Sixteen.

"You've got protection. I gave you one for your birthday." She reached inside her open shirt without looking away from him and undid her bra in the front. Light glimmered on the fragile hook behind the bow. "I got it from Susan Templeton, so you know it's new."

It was true. He carried Susan's condom in his wallet like a compass. He'd unwrapped the tiny gift too carefully, too slowly (it was closed with a bow) because Luce's shining eyes had urged him to hurry and he'd wanted to drive her nuts, and when the little latex package lay in his palm on its wrapping paper the thrill of it arrowed to his groin. But at the same time, the excitement was colored with sadness. That part of the game was over. The tingle of sexual electricity that made his veins hum day and night and in his dreams now had voltage.

This *was* complicated, *did* need language. He hadn't even sorted it out completely in his own head. Every part of him stretched with wanting her. But—and this made him ashamed for some reason—he hoped to keep his virginity, that feeling of purity he'd already lived through at the altar, and in direct contradiction to *that,* which made everything still more confusing, he was hoping if he delayed long enough he'd jump into a future when they were doing it somewhere nicer than the back of a pickup truck, and he could bring that learning back here and put it to use. But Louise's death should have taught him that there's never a benefit in knowing what's to come.

"Joe. *Now.*" She pulled the two halves of her cotton workshirt open and dropped it off her shoulders, and then the two halves of her bra, which glowed as if the moon were ultraviolet, and then, with her arms caught in straps and sleeves, she stood up and balanced barefoot in the runnels to shake herself free.

Oh, Jesus. His hands without any directions from his brain tugged on the fringe of her cutoffs and they fell around her ankles. A little bow on the front of her panties matched the one on her bra. And the one on his gift two weeks ago, he realized. Did women really expect men to notice such things, or did they do it for themselves?

He fumbled for his wallet while she bent to undo his jeans. He had his hands on the leather for a moment before it skidded open out of his hands and into a corner of the pickup bed.

"Leave it," she said.

He shook his head, but she was over him now, on top of him, her hands everywhere at once, and he was paralyzed. Even free of the weight of her, he would be incapable of moving to get it. A man at such times is no better than a 'possum in the headlights.

She was having trouble getting his jeans off, even though he'd abdicated and was doing what he could to help. "Caught on something," she said, giggling. She put a hand on his chest and pushed, banging his head on the tailgate hard enough that his vision blurred, but it didn't slow her a bit. "There, now," she finally said, the warmth of her exertion in her face and his.

There, now. They'd been playing at this for years, finding the wooded spots a truck could get to, a hand, a finger could get to, and they'd skinny-dipped more than a few times in her pool late at night with the lights off, too near in his mind to her parents' bedroom window for safety, but in the back of the truck on the blanket under half a moon, hot and laughing and naked, *there, now.*

As it turned out, he didn't need instructions from the future. The diagrams are hardwired in the brain or muscles, or both. They knew each other so well that the clumsiness he was terrified of happened only in the clothes-shucking phase; after that, rolled in the blanket, it was as if they'd been making love for years. And they had been, in their heads. Or he had, anyway.

"I guess you're never going to murmur sweet nothings in my ear, huh?"

He kissed it instead. They sat against the truck cab now, holding hands on their thighs under the blanket, looking past the leaves and tree shapes at the stars.

"What's this?" She moved her foot, dragging something with it, reached down and came up with the condom. She held it up so he could see it. "Better use this," she said.

Too late for that.

Oh. By the time they had it figured out and in place, it wasn't.

"Susan has lots of them," she said on the drive home.

Joseph didn't need to ask lots of what.

"But I'm thinking we should have our own supply. So nobody else can count."

Makes sense.

"And I'm not the brazen slut Susan is." She gave it a two-count. "Am I?"

He braked, stopping the truck in the middle of the road, slipped it into neutral, and leaned over and kissed her gently for a long time. He put the truck in gear again, and after a while she softly said, "I didn't think so."

The lights were still on at her house when they pulled up, so they sat out front at the curb in the dark truck and waited.

"Put the cab light on," Luce said. "That way they'll know we're not fooling around out here." He could hear her smile.

They sat comfortably without talking for a long time, something they were better at than almost any couple on earth. She reached for the door handle only after the living-room lights went out and the bedroom lights came on. "It's probably a silly thing," she told him, "but if I wait until they've gone to bed, I feel freer, even though they know we're sitting here, and know I know they know." She giggled again. It was a giggling night. "Besides, Mom would take one look at me tonight and guess everything." She kissed him lightly on the forehead, as if he were still a friend. "Good-night, honey."

Mrs. Sears might know everything anyway when she saw Luce at breakfast in the morning. Joseph was pretty sure that both of them were wearing something unseen—like that kiss on his forehead that must be shining like a tattoo. They'd slipped into new skins. He shifted into neutral and let the truck coast.

How could he live at home now? He felt crowded by this new closeness. *At nineteen,* he thought, *it's time to get my own place.* The job he had driving for Parker paid enough, and at the end of the summer he'd be awarded his diploma, a year and a half late and half a year behind Luce.

She'd made him go back for it. "I don't mind that you want to work in the dirt your whole life," she'd said. "You're good at it. You're helping build houses and change landscapes. But in this life you fill squares, and right now the square you have to fill is high school. Everybody needs it for any decent future." He should've—but didn't—have the facts to disagree with her, which is partly why she won. "There's a program of classes in the evenings and weekends and summers; I've checked. You can make up the year you lost when you quit. I'm not going to fill out forms years from now and under *husband's education* check *none*."

Joseph found he liked math, that a language of symbols came naturally to him, and that a minimum effort in the other courses would garner low Cs, good enough to get what she—and now he—wanted. He signed up for a drawing class to fill the one required elective, and there too the language was symbols, pictures, and his teacher unearthed a rough talent that excited both of them. In charcoal on rough paper, he captured the creatures in the swamp—the dragonflies, the snakes, the occasional alligator—and once while he was sitting at an easel his teacher had laid a hand on his arm for balance, leaned over and smudged the drawing with the meat of his hand, and said, "Now that wing's moving; that thing's *alive*." For his final project, he'd cut some reeds in the swamp and brought to class a slab of slate the size of a magazine. He pestled clods of red ochre in a mortar and when he had a powder put two fingerfuls of it in his mouth and worked it with his spit into a spray. Snapping turtle on a mudbank. Heron watching. *That's me,* he'd thought: *a turtle in the mud being watched by a thin, winged predator.* Each octagonal ocellus in the turtle's shell grew like a tiny flower. The same color as the mud, it looked like holes, like lace. *Like Time,* he thought. *Like that carpet.* He went back later and rimmed each one in black and blew the footprints and the heron's eye at the same time. The heron's feathers he didn't paint; he left them imagined in the stone, their natural color.

When Luce had sent him back to school (what other way was there to say it?), and he'd obeyed (that too couldn't be said another way), and he'd liked it, he had known he would marry her after he graduated. How he'd ask her, he didn't know. In his mind, it would require a persuasive argument, and while she sometimes understood him perfectly, she sometimes chose not to.

He could almost but not quite coast from Luce's house to his own. He turned the engine over for the last fifty yards and turned it off again when the truck bumped up into the driveway. *Then there's the folks,* he thought, looking at the house lights. *I'm getting married, moving out.* Try saying that—and all that lay underneath it—with your hands. *But I guess now's the time.* His mouth had that same sticky taste it had gotten when he'd finished painting. He hitched up his pants. *Manhood.*

His mother and dad were still up, in the living room watching a late movie. His four-year-old brother, Louis, was stretched out asleep on the floor at their feet like a dog. This wasn't a future he'd seen, but he suddenly knew it would play out exactly as he'd just half imagined it while walking to the front door (he could have imagined it in all its detail if he had tried, he thought; *he could call the future into being at his whim*): Mother glanced up to say hello and stopped with the word lying unsaid on her tongue. Which of the invisible signs he was wearing did she see? She put her hand on her husband's and tapped it twice, to tell him to pay attention.

Here it comes, love's aftermath.

"Have a nice night, dear?"

The last small doubt gone, he nodded. God hadn't put a mark on Cain for all men to see because he'd killed his brother; he'd marked him later, for getting laid, so Eve could see it.

"What did you do?"

The first time, Mother, she sat on top of me. The second time, well—he couldn't help but smile. Joseph cranked a movie camera, an anachronism, the old charades sign.

Her eyes flicked to her wristwatch.

He moved a steering wheel a quarter of an inch in each direction.

Frank was alerted now, though about what he wasn't sure, and he focused on Joseph's eyes. Both of them knew Helen's interrogation tactics well enough to know that the prisoner broke first with an eyelid's flutter, a tic. Joseph's eyelid, on cue, began to jump.

"I hope to God you took him out to that treehouse," Helen told her husband. In answer to his blank look she said, "To talk about sex."

"Maybe it's not—"

"You and Luce," she said, not even a question.

That she thought she had a right to know in the first place angered him more. You could have kept this knowledge to yourself, Mother.

Keep control. Just tell 'em what you've got to tell 'em. He touched his ring finger.

"You tell *her* that?"

No.

"Well, that's something anyway."

"Will you two slow down?" Frank had missed the finger sign.

"Your son and your neighbor's daughter are all grown up," she said as if she were talking to a child, "and now Joseph thinks he has to marry her."

Your neighbor's daughter. A traveling salesman goes up to a farmhouse and knocks on the door, which is answered by the neighbor's daughter. . . .

"Is that right, son? The part about marriage, I mean. The rest"—he took his hand out from under Helen's—"isn't our business."

"Whose business is it, then?"

"Theirs."

"Ours."

"It wasn't your parents' business when we did it," Frank said.

"Frank!"

"At the lake." He would have winked at his son, if he had the nerve, but that was lacking.

"We had an understanding," she said. Tears were starting. "We always knew we'd be married."

Joseph beat on his chest for their attention, and when he had it left a finger on his breastbone.

"You too," his father said.

Joseph nodded and held up five fingers.

"For five minutes?" his mother said.

"Five months," his father corrected.

He pulled his hands slowly apart. *Five years.* He looked at his hands in the air, noticed they were clenched, and forced them open and down to his sides. Why is everybody mad at everybody?

"That's not so hard to believe, Helen, if you think about it," his father said. "When have you seen them apart?" Be glad, Frank thought, that this isn't what drove Joseph out of high school, that they haven't been working like rabbits for years making us grandparents. Something clicked. "Did Luce have anything to do with your going back to finish your education?"

Thank you, Dad.

"See?" he said to his wife.

So he's defended her before. Why does my mother hate the woman I love? She's a nice girl.

"She's a nice girl," Frank said.

"Not a girl any longer," Helen reminded him.

And your son's not a boy.

"And our son's no longer a boy."

Well, why not just go upstairs and let his father finish the argument for him?

That silence stayed palpable for what seemed five minutes until his father broke it. "I don't know if this is a good time or a bad time," Frank said, standing, "but we're both in so much trouble with your mother right now, Son,

I'd just as soon get hung for a sheep as a lamb. Or hung once instead of twice—or something."

I think it's *hanged,* Dad. Something Luce had said.

"What are you talking about, Frank?"

"Give me a minute."

His dad went into the den, leaving the two to stare at each other. His mother's eyes were filled and sore-looking.

"This was going to be a graduation present in a couple of months," Frank said, handing the papers to Joseph.

"Frank?"

"I bought it back, Helen." To Joseph he said, "That miserable piece of swampland you love so much is yours."

Helen came out of her chair like a rocket, and both men stiffened without the time for thought first, expecting blows, but she kissed her husband violently and hugged her son and wept. The weeping—she did it with loud hiccups—woke Louis, who sat up rubbing his eyes and looking peeved.

Over his mother's shaking shoulders, Joseph eyed his father, who shrugged. *You'll find out about women soon enough,* his look said. *But it won't do you any good.*

He thought he'd learned all he needed in the back of the pickup with Luce, but he was wrong. He took the deed upstairs to bed and put it under his pillow, where he'd kept his treasures as a child. Since he was very young he had known that what was under his head helped shape his dreams. It worked this time too; when he awoke he had a picture of the house he wanted, even to the views out its windows.

At dawn on Sunday, with the deed, a packed lunch, a compass, a tape, and a shovel, he stood on the boundary of his land and his neighbors' and watched the sun light up the trees as if they were candles. When it had cleared their tops, he started in.

A road could be forced into these trees in only two spots. At the first, he'd be in the marsh immediately, and knew anyway that there would never be enough light. But from the other spot he could put in a drive that would curve and climb slowly, drain well, and end on a level place large enough for a house. Those cedars—there and there—would have to come down, as would some of the chalk maples for the road, and maybe one of the oaks, but cedar was the wood he wanted anyway: almost as good as hemlock, hard to work, smelly, but impervious to any insect God had yet invented. And oak and maple were good for burning. He knew this land from memory but walked it again with a house in the center of it in his mind's eye and gained a new appreciation for the slant and physical weight of the light, and he squatted from time to time so his hands and feet could hold the soil. He sifted it through fingers and toes like powder. *A good place.*

He laid out a rough square, forty by forty, a diamond, really, against the future road, and staked the corners with a cedar's fallen branches. Six—maybe five—of the old-growth trees would have to come down. That sixth he might leave in the wall. He sat on the carpet of shed needles, but not needles exactly, waiting out the sun's arc and hour by hour liking more the place he had chosen. It was full of squirrels and bright birds and the chatter of life. When the long shadows started, he went home to tell Luce.

She didn't accept the news with joy.

"I have this right, don't I? Your father bought the Swamp?" She always gave it a capital.

Yes.

"The *Swamp?*"

How can she not know I love it?

"And then he gave it to you."

To us. A wedding present, but you don't know that yet.

"And then—and here's the part I don't think I'm clear on—you want to *live* there?"

Since I can remember.

"Not near it? *In* it?"

You've been there, Luce. It's magical.

"You're going to make a house there."

With a garage and a garden and a picket fence if you want one. But his own happiness was leaking away.

She zeroed in. "It'll be like building the Panama Canal," she said. "Mud and ick and bugs and disease.

Mosquitoes and yellow fever. A 'gator'll drag you under, and I'll never see you again."

As happens, the heart remembered only the last part: *I'll never see you again.* A sadness like a puncture ached. He got up to go.

"Stay for dinner," she said. "I think Mom knows."

He shook his head and went out.

The construction site was a different place now. Parker & Son (the Son half of the company absent, never really present, as Lonnie and his father had silently agreed) went about its business of hauling, from one side of the plat to the other, yards of pit run or gravel or top-soil, of carrying to the municipal dump the remnants of material that went into the building of houses, but Joseph no longer saw any of it as excess, as refuse, only the ingredients he needed. He began stockpiling what he could use, or even what he thought, given the right circumstances, he might one day use. Any sizable block of wood that measured more than a couple of feet. Half sheets of drywall. Odd lengths of galvanized pipe. Spool ends and bird's nests of electrical wire. Insulation. Warped, forgotten, or mis-sawn two-by-fours. Bundles of rebar. Bricks. Paving stones. Sheets of shale and lumps of broken concrete the machines sometimes pulled up from God knew what earlier constructions.

Parker thought the concrete a bit much. Joseph was eyeing it suspiciously, half tempted to put it back, when Parker joined him at the end of the day.

"I thought at first you were going to open a cut-rate builder's supply, but even the crooks I know wouldn't try to put in old concrete."

Joseph put on a wry smile and nodded.

"You've got two loads here, maybe three, that we're not getting paid to carry."

Another nod.

"And I don't know how many hours of sorting and stacking you've done that I've already paid you for. I have, haven't I?"

A third nod.

"That's bad business on my part."

Joseph's smile was gone now. It hadn't seemed to him like theft, but he guessed it was.

"I'm not too concerned about any of that, though," Parker said. "Or, anyway, not as much as I am about *you*. You've grown into a packrat, and you ought to be fifty or sixty years away from that yet. Wait 'til you're my age, at least, for criminy's sake."

Joseph thought about how to respond to that. He had lots of options, the easiest being another nod and let it go. But he dug into his wallet and unfolded a page-sized square of drawing paper and spread it out on the Diamond Reo's running board. He weighted one end with his keys and the other with his wallet and stepped back.

Parker bent over it for a long time, then held it up so the light glanced off it at an angle that made it easier to read, then refolded it carefully along its creases and handed it back to Joseph. "Got the property?" he asked.

Best in the world.

"Show it to me?"

They drove home in their two trucks, bumper to tailgate because Parker didn't know where he was being led, and Joseph took him into the woods a couple of blocks from Parker's house, where it was now nearly dusk, although the outside still had an hour of afternoon left.

Parker absentmindedly raised one of the lot corners that had fallen and gently screwed it back into its soil. "I wanted to do this too, when I was your age," he said. "But I never got up the gumption." He turned on his heel slowly and did some mental figuring. "Nice lot; good, simple house design." He nodded, as if finally persuaded that he agreed with himself. "But you can't use half that crap you've collected."

Two days later Joseph arrived at the job site to find his pile in two: one neatly stacked; one a heap.

One of Parker's friends loaned Joseph a backhoe on Sundays, thinking he was the Son in Parker &. "If your boy needs a backhoe, sure, he can use this one," the man had said, and Parker hadn't corrected him. With it, Joseph was able to cut the road. A bulldozer would have been quicker. He felled an oak or a chalk maple or a cedar with a chainsaw each afternoon before his night class and on

Sunday used the backhoe to drag them to the sides, where on other nights he cut each up into fireplace lengths. When the house was finished, he'd buy an ax and split them. And no matter what Luce thought of the project now, he knew she'd live in the house with him someday, and he was more than a little curious to see how he would manage that.

At the moment, she hated the whole idea. He'd been missing dates or had been late for them for two months, and all he had to show for it was a gouge in the earth and some dead trees. "What girl wants to come in second to this?"

They were standing where the bedroom would be.

"After we made love, you seemed to lose interest." She tagged him on the arm, almost but not quite playfully. "Mom warned me guys'll do that, but I thought she was lying."

He reached for her breasts to show his interest, but she danced back.

"Oh, no, you don't. I was a week late after that first time and nearly had a heart attack—"

Heart attack triggers it. The trees and shadows dissolve, and he thinks *Alka-Seltzer* because they're giving up their heft like bubbles and behind him is a fizzing. Long after the fact, like echoes, the scream of metal and the smell of rubber and the bleat of a horn hit the back of his skull like fists. He's on the street in front of his parents' house, and he knows when he turns he will see an accident at the Allisenis' curb. It all happens very slowly, as if underwater, and he's terrified but doesn't know why. Something damaged falls and rattles. Someone moans. He still hasn't made the full turn.

His mother is at the door with her hands to her mouth, and he's turning, turning *(go faster! faster!)* away from her to see. The back of the car's in sight: a pickup he doesn't recognize, one lifted four feet by huge tires, but that means nothing; it might not be built yet, or if built, not bought.

Mrs. Alliseni is standing on one shoe in the middle of the street, her hand in the air as if hailing a cab. Stopping a car. Holding a steering wheel. Buying a drink. It's broken, he realizes. Her face is masked with shock or alcohol.

He keeps turning, pivoting like a weathervane in a zephyr. *Hurry.* The front of the next car is small and blue. The pavement glints with broken glass and shiny fluids. He identifies their sources by their colors: green, black, blue; radiator, oil pan, windshield-washer reservoir.

A baby cries in one impossibly long breath, and it's joined by his mother, now behind him, and then time unlocks itself and he can move.

That's Luce at the wheel, her forehead against the horn, her hair spilling like a blonde waterfall from the driver's window. Beside her, a silhouette behind the starred windshield, the profile of his father moves. The baby's cry—

"—when I thought I was knocked up." Luce caught a bothersome strand of hair with her teeth and half turned her back to him. "You agreed to buy condoms, but I have to keep getting them from Susan."

(He'd tried to buy them, although he didn't think of that now. Condoms weren't shelved where a young man or woman could pick them up and carry them to the checkout; for some reason they hung on displays behind the counter in reach only of a dour, middle-aged woman, and he had no way of asking for them except in signs. What sign could he possibly devise that wouldn't get him arrested?)

He rather stupidly expected the hard ground to be muddy and lifted one foot as if he were standing in a puddle.

"Well?"

Joseph took a step and gathered her to him, her soft hair and curves and clothes with their odors of soap and perfume and cedar fronds. She struggled for half a minute, but he gripped her like a vine. He tasted her with his nose and palms, kneading the place on the back of her neck that collected the scent of her hair until she went limp in his arms and he had to let her slide free, down, like pouring oil.

From where she lay, Luce could see the last of the light green the tops of the blue-black cedars over Joseph's bare shoulders. Her hips' rhythmic rocking made it pulse. A gust blew a storm of cottonwood seed that settled like dandelions in their hair and damp skin and carpeted their not-yet-built bedroom in fluff. She fell in love twice, each for the second time.

"All I wanted was an apology," she said. They were side by side now on their backs. "But this will do."

Joseph rested a hand on the ridge of her pelvic bone, balancing his palm on it, and as if the warmth of it there completed something, she said, "I'm pregnant."

He sat up.

"Just now."

He started to lift his hand, but she held it where it was.

"It's all right. It's more than all right; it's wonderful."

So he worked harder. He bribed, with half a dozen cases of beer, a crew that poured slabs to help him with the foundation, and what would have taken him weeks alone he got done in a morning. *With enough hands you can build pyramids.* He hooked his sewer up illegally, not wanting to wait for the paperwork, counting on Parker's friendship with the inspector, a former contractor himself whose favorite response to trouble was, "It's easier to obtain forgiveness than permission." *We'll see.* He drove cedar footers into the cement with a gun that used explosive nails, the gun and nails lent to him by a framer Parker knew. On the Sunday he began framing, a crew of ten arrived and gave him a barn raising. They put up his walls in four hours.

"Tell us when the joists get here," the framer said, "and we'll give you a roof."

When they'd driven away, Parker stood with Joseph in the house's ribs, Parker with his hand on the tree Joseph had managed in the end, with professional help, to save in a wall. "Got the money for joists?"

Joseph shook his head. He'd expected not to get that far for six months.

"I'll give you an advance. Get 'em out here Sunday?"

Better make it two Sundays, to be safe.

"See you back here then," Parker said.

Joseph put his hand out to shake, and Parker took it, then pulled the boy close for a hug.

A drugstore test proved Luce's knowledge right. "Baby's first test," Luce said, holding up the stick. "Maybe I'll start an album."

House job diapers crib clothes doctors furniture roof washer dryer bed stove lights refrigerator bills television car hospital. You can never own—you can never drive—a small blue car. Don't go anywhere with my dad. Stay off that street entirely until our daughter's grown.

"What shall we name him?"

He put a hand on his hip, struck a pose. Her.

"Him. He's a boy."

No, he's not.

"Pick a name that goes both ways, then."

Francis. Robin. Alex. Chris. He shook his head.

"Jo. We'll add an e when the time comes."

His parents had subtracted one.

Her eyes told him he had to do this thing now. Joseph had wanted to wait and do it right, with flowers and music, but time had taught him that Time decides. His father had said it once: Man plans; God laughs. He opened the toolbox in the truckbed and sorted through the little plastic drawers until he found O rings the right size. He pushed one onto her finger and kissed it. *Black rubber, three for nineteen cents. Fits on the end of hydraulic hoses. Lose it, I've got a couple dozen more.* Had any man ever done any worse?

Luce held her hand out at arm's length like a horrible echo of Mrs. Alliseni. She admired the ring on her finger for a moment, as if the light were refracting from it instead of getting sucked in and lost, then smiled at him. She undid the top button of her blouse, reached inside, and took out the whistle. "We've been engaged for nearly six years," she said. "Didn't you know?"

The house had a roof. He'd tacked down the felt paper but didn't have the money for shingles. He'd muscled on the lower half of an outside wall, three-eighths-inch plywood sheets that he'd need help to finish. Plastic plumbing starts were anchored in the bare concrete floor. He'd firmed out the door and window openings with cedar, decided it was habitable enough for one, and moved in.

Joseph had wanted to sleep in the swamp since Louise was alive, so it wasn't too surprising that he thought of her the first night. She came with the rain. It started as drizzle that lasted all day, slicking up the red clay and making the Diamond Reo difficult and dangerous to handle, then just before quitting time it started coming down in sheets. The road he'd built carried the water off nicely, just as he'd planned, but he kept imagining Louise's reflection by lightning in the pools that were forming. The rain thrummed on the roof, and he wished for the hammer of tin and decided he'd do it; it was cheaper, in any case, and easy to get. He lay down in his clothes and on the spares he'd brought, sticky with the humidity that had settled over the town for months. He stared out the empty places where windows would go and listened to the rumble of the thunderstorm move off, leaving its rain behind. And her. She answered an owl with her own voice, and he fell asleep waiting for her to visit, to call his name.

A cry in the night woke him from a horrible dream. In it he could move backward in the future and fix whatever was to come that hadn't happened yet, but he couldn't travel into any part of his past. He had stood at a gate, the present, trying to grasp Louise's tiny hands through thick bars as if she were a prisoner and he her visitor, knowing while he did it that if he somehow managed to pull her through to this side there was no place for her.

The cry came again. It sounded human, skipping across the water. Perhaps a night bird hunting now that the rain had stopped. He went out and relieved himself, as far from the house as memory allowed, reminding himself to have the water connected so he could buy a toilet. He lay down on his bed of clothes again but thought he didn't sleep.

"Joe."

It felt like another dream. The sun was up; he was late for work. Luce was kneeling beside him, her hand on his shoulder, an awfulness plain in her face.

"Are you awake?"

He was, but when? He saw through the interior studs that the bathroom was still without a toilet.

"I think the baby died. Oh, Joe—" She took his hands but instead of drawing closer sat back on her heels. "I had a pain in the night, a big cramp, and then I felt different inside."

Maybe gas, Joseph hoped, or something peculiar to women, but was ashamed of that thought.

"The same way I knew I had a baby, I know I don't. I'm going into the doctor's this morning. Will you come?"

He walked her to the place she'd parked under the cedars, and in that light under those trees her small white car looked blue.

"Oh," she said, sliding in behind the wheel, "by the way. Your parents are throwing a party for your graduation next week, and my parents are having one for our engagement. Saturday night, both of them. Isn't that great? Won't it be fun? Two parties." She turned the key savagely. "Somewhere in between them maybe the two of us can find the time to fit in a funeral."

She began to close the door, but he held it open, pushed her gently over into the passenger's seat, and took the wheel in his hands. *I'll drive.*

She had lost the baby. It was nothing she did, the doctor told them, and nothing she didn't do. She put her hands on Luce's. "When this happens this early, in the first trimester, it's best the pregnancy doesn't continue. It's hard, but please trust me when I say it would be harder on both of you—the three of you, on everybody—if you'd carried this baby to term. There's no reason I can see that you can't have another when you're ready."

"I'll never be ready again," Luce said.

"Yes, you will." Her physician, whom Joseph knew only as Margaret, pulled Luce to her feet until they stood toe to toe, still holding hands. It looked like the beginnings of a dance, he thought. "I've been your doctor since you were just a girl, Luce; you have to listen to me now. These things happen. The pain you're feeling will go. The memory of it mightn't, but the pain will."

Luce bowed her head to avoid Margaret's eyes. Joseph wished there was room between them or beside them for him, but there wasn't, so he stayed in his seat.

"Look at me, sweetheart."

Luce shook her head. She was crying, Joseph saw.

"Look at me."

Joseph heard the Witch. He came up halfway in his chair, which broke a spell for Luce. She did something with her hands, a twisting flourish and a sort of patty-cake finish, and then she was free of her doctor and wheeling toward the door. On her way past him she shoved him down again until he was sitting and she was, just that suddenly, gone.

He started to rise a second time, but Margaret gently put a hand on his shoulder and made him sit. "Let her go," she said. "She'll want you later, but not now."

Her advice collided with his instinct, but he did as she told him and stayed. And even as he did, settling back into the chair again, his hands on its skinny arms, Joseph wondered how that had happened so easily. *It's her voice,* he decided after a moment. *What a terrific weapon it is that I don't own.*

Dr. Margaret sat at her own desk and moved a sheaf of papers on it page by page, and Joseph thought that he was meant to sit and wait and nothing more, so for a third time his muscles bunched to stand.

She interrupted the action. "You know," she said without looking up, "Luce is—has always been, for that matter—the kind of girl I wish *my* son had fallen for, the kind of woman I'd want as a friend. We dropped the *doctor* between us a long time ago." She looked up then, locked her gaze on his, and smiled. "But it's *your* friendship that's necessary."

Joseph nodded, a little angrily.

"I mean it. Not your love, not even your willingness to sit around and listen to her blubber, if that's what she wants to do, but your friendship; the fact that you *like* her is going to make the difference now. And later."

This time he didn't nod but stared.

"It's the later that worries me most," she said quietly. "When Luce looks back on this, and she will, Joseph, she'll replay like a movie everything you did and—"

Said?

She sat straighter. "Well, you two must have ways of talking. And she'll remember it all. She's taking this very hard for a pregnancy so new."

Joseph stood finally and touched the outside corner of his eye where it met his temple. His shorthand for *I know. And I know how to be Luce's friend without anybody's help.* He was standing in the hallway outside her office before he wondered if he did.

Joseph had been in this hospital so many times before and after this moment that the walk from Luce's doctor's office down to the ground floor and the parking lot should have been easy, but he got lost, even following the color-coded tape (yellow for lobby) glued to the linoleum tiles. He rode an elevator down into the emergency room, and the doors opened onto screaming.

Dr. Higgerby arrived at the same time, but from the parking lot, called by the resident to consult on a case that perplexed her. She was puzzling over that screaming man, who stopped yelling only long enough to take another long breath, but she could find no wounds. He was dirty, stripped almost naked, sitting on a steel examination table, and hollering. She'd been over his body twice carefully and was beginning the third tour with a lighted magnifying glass as Higgerby hurried past him, putting a hitch in his gait, a sort of walking double-take, when he saw Joseph.

"You okay?" he asked, only slowing.

Joseph nodded. Sure; I'm lost is all.

"Don't go anywhere. I'll be back."

Joseph stared at his huge retreating back, the cloth of his suit coat stretched like a plaid sail across it. The screaming went on and on, crawling up the bone marrow like a trail of ants and nesting at the sides of the bottom of the skull just below the ears. He found a chair and covered his head with his hands.

Higgerby hadn't yet touched the resident's patient. Joseph watched his gestures—pointing here and there, making a complicated sign that denoted an instrument or procedure—and watched the resident's reactions to his question: lifting the man's arm, probing his armpit and then his abdomen, shining a light in his eye. Finally Higgerby prescribed something, or agreed with a prescription, and a needle was put into the man's arm and the screaming stopped.

Higgerby shifted from one foot to the other until they'd wheeled him out, then came over. "Are you sure you're all right? What are you doing here?"

Joseph touched his ring finger.

"Your hand's hurt?"

No. He made an L with his thumb and finger.

"Luce? Where is she?"

Joseph shrugged.

"What's wrong?"

Higgerby hadn't let Joseph chase him away five years before. He'd driven home from the funeral parlor, stewing about what he'd said and done, wishing he had said *this* instead, wishing he'd done *that* when he'd had the chance, slapping his hand on the dashboard from time to time to emphasize important points in the argument with himself. Then he'd dreamed for two nights in a row of Joseph's contorted face through the glass of the windshield (the wipers going, for some reason, contorting the features further), that screech real in his ears even in the dream, and that had convinced him to try again.

For a while he'd courted the boy, bringing gifts: a slingshot, a fishing pole, even a bicycle once. They'd managed something like friendship, finally, at least he thought they had, but even after all these years it was Higgerby who had to make the moves, had to come by the house with baseball tickets or some such, begging.

Higgerby thought that Joseph had never quite lost the suspicion that he was being studied, and Higgerby had to admit that he supposed it was true. The kid—kid no longer—fascinated him.

"Anything I can do?"

Joseph shook his head.

"That other fellow, he's difficult," Higgerby said, acknowledging the rejection. "Can't find anything wrong with him. Got him sedated for everybody else's peace of mind, so we could hear ourselves think. Now, then. I feel like going fishing."

Now's a bad time, Doc.

"Not this weekend?"

Joseph extended a thumb and little finger and held them to his ear. I'll call you.

Higgerby laughed. "Right."

But Joseph did call the next day—or rather had Luce call for him—to invite him to the party.

All parties everywhere, Joseph thought, were horrible, but they were worse when they were for you, and worse still when the heart didn't want one. In the early stages of such affairs, when the guests were still sober, they mostly left him alone, and that was all right—he'd eavesdrop, making mental notes of the gossip that was worth the effort of passing on to Luce—but after a couple of hours they talked to him and at him without mercy. His eyes would freeze over, and he'd do something fast with his fingers (it didn't matter what, even if it was rude; the talker was drunk) and turn his back and try to escape. He'd gathered, through the years, a dozen or so great lines—*killing shots*—he wished he could deliver.

Luce loved parties, usually, with the same passion that Joseph hated them, and was skilled in maneuvering guests and conversations, even his mother, who liked Luce enormously but was always clumsy around her. Luce turned her seemingly innocent comment, "It must be lovely, this time of year, to have a pool," into a discussion of chlorine and electric bills—"What does it cost us, Mom?" she asked her mother, Linda—and while Joseph could have struck himself in the forehead for not understanding earlier, Luce and Linda nudged her from that line of thinking to how nicely the Tafts had landscaped their backyard, having understood all along.

Luce even remembered all of his relatives' names, and with a fixed smile that only Joseph knew was fixed listened to boring reminiscences about their silent and rather strange nephew, cousin, grandson, and added, when she was given the opportunity, some often fabricated anecdote of her own. She smiled through all of it. Nobody knew about the baby's start, and none knew now about its end. She wore the black, beveled, rubber O ring next to the inexpensive real one he'd bought her, and he couldn't tell which she liked best.

At ten o'clock, as agreed, the party moved down the street to the Sears house. Their dining-room table was piled with wrapped packages—blenders and towels and toasters and such—but also with money in small white envelopes like the ones passed around in church, and best of all, from both fathers, gift certificates to the local builder's supply. *Kitchen*, one said. *Bathroom*, said the other. *Bathtubs and toilets and sinks and stoves and refrigerators.*

Luce's father, Luke, leaning on a cane, cleared his throat and rather apologetically announced that everybody had agreed to bring wedding presents to the engagement party. "You might need this stuff sooner," he said. Joseph looked for his mother to see if she was watching them open the gifts, but she was in the backyard, at the umbrella table by the pool, drinking.

Luce had to give a speech for the two of them, and Joseph, having drunk more than he was used to, stood behind her and pantomimed, in a terrible parody of Sign, to an imaginary deaf audience. Luce was confused at the laughter, particularly because each time she turned around to see if he understood, Joseph was smiling benignly.

"When's the date?" one of her relatives asked.

"When is it?"

The crowd took it up: "When? When? When? When?"

Luce only smiled and shrugged, then looked to Joseph for help.

Conspiracy, he thought. He took her hand, and they quieted.

He let the muscles in his face go still, then curled a lip into a grimace that became a rictus, slowly grew a hump on his back, and held up a hand that withered into a claw.

"Halloween!" Linda shouted, clapping her hands as if she were a child.

On the nose. The small crowd cheered.

Luce, in spite of her pain or because of it, was delighted too, and bringing her joy tonight delighted Joseph. He wondered if she guessed he'd chosen the date only because it was one he could say.

"I need your help with the guest list," she'd said, and he'd turned away. "Don't do that, please, Joseph." She slid a piece of paper in front of him. "Just write down the names of those you want."

She, like his mother, never gave up trying this; it was as if the two of them thought he were keeping an interesting new form of handwriting a secret from humanity.

He pushed the page back and signed from the heart, *Thank you.*

"Thanks for what?"

He tapped the sheet.

"Oh. The thank-you notes. That list?"

He nodded. Plus two.

"Who?"

He held his hand horizontal, moved it vertical: dump truck.

"Just him? Not the missus?"

Joseph shook his head. He wondered what division he had caused in that family but knew it wasn't something he could fix. The time when he and Lonnie could have been friends had passed, somehow, with a look or an action—or an action untaken—on his part, or on Lonnie's. The few times he had seen the mother, she had pretended he hadn't.

"Who's the second one?"

He puffed his cheeks out.

"Dr. Higgerby. Of course. We invited him, but he couldn't come." She made a note. "Maybe we should scatter some of my relatives onto your side."

He grinned at her, having already seen that she wouldn't.

The Rev Roy officiated. He had a connection to Luce's family too, something to do with her father's damaged leg, a hunting accident. Perhaps the man sniffed out pain. He cradled the Bible in that hand that had once disgusted and attracted Joseph. Behind them the organist coughed and rustled, flipping through her pages of music, preparing in the beginning for the end.

"You two ready?" The Rev Roy asked.

Luce nodded.

The Rev Roy cleared his throat. "People of God," he said, "welcome to my house, your house, the house of the Lord. You don't come near often enough."

A laugh or two, from the bride's side, which is what he wanted. *Tell me again, Luce, why we chose him?*

"Now, I've married lots of folks, white and black, young and old, and I do it a bit differently. I take some time with it, as God asks. We don't hurry into this life, and we don't hurry into this. The couple, here, Joseph and Luce—as fine a young man and woman as I know—are going to stand up here a little while with me, their backs straight out of nervousness and pride, fainting perhaps unless they get the blood moving" (to them, *sotto voce,* he said, "Bend your knees a little") "while I talk for a bit about the two of them, and marrying, and life. You see, God's hand is plain in this; they met in disaster and turned it into love.

"I told this young man here, years ago in the time of his family's tragedy, that my father had rebuilt this hand"—he held it up, clutching the Bible—"with hammer and tongs. Made new again, with the tools of man, what a horse had destroyed. *Fixed God's work*. And I promised I'd tell him about it, but I never got the chance. He never came back to listen to the story, but he's here now, and can't leave."

More laughs. Fine for the audience.

The Rev Roy nodded, encouraging them. "You can laugh. This is a happy day. There's nothing but smiles in this house this morning. There's nothing but joy for these two here." He brought the book down, blessing them in passing. "But now that story.

"I was where I shouldn't, too near a young horse my father was shoeing, even though I knew better, had been told not to, that this animal was skittish as well as bad-tempered. My father and I were diagonal from each other, the horse in between us, and he thought I'd listened and had left when he'd said, and when that horse reared up my father moved him with a hip, to kick and paw at air, he thought, but no! that horse struck at *me*. His forehoof hit my hand like a dull ax and split it open."

The Rev Roy looked at his hand, remembering, it seemed to the audience, but Joseph could see it was only for effect.

"Well, I hollered. I thought I was dying. I bawled from fear of that great beast in a rage as much as from the pain I was just starting to feel, and I yelled with surprise at seeing my blood where it shouldn't be, geysering out of that wound, spraying the shoulder of the horse and making him more crazy.

"I heard my father's hammer ring on the ground and then saw an arm snake around that block of muscle that's a horse's neck, and he threw him! *He threw him!* And he lifted me with his free hand as if I weighed no more than his coffee cup.

"My father was a big man."

An appreciative chuckle. Joseph moved his feet in his shoes to feel them.

"But not *that* big. I was seven and a half, and not small even then. That horse—well, he was a *horse*. You get my meaning here, people? No *man* can do such things, not even a father bent on protecting his children. He clamped a hand around the wound and stanched the flow like a spigot had been turned.

"Mama's in the yard now, don't you know? 'What have you done to my baby?' she says, or words like those. 'Horse stepped on the boy,' my father says, 'but you can't blame the horse.' The horse has got to its feet by now, and my father turns to it the way he'd face an enemy and punches it between the eyes. He's got a fist like a splitting maul, and it goes down again, shaking its head, groggy and bewildered. 'Don't blame the horse,' he says again, perhaps to himself this time. 'Blame the boy for bein' where I told him not to.'

"He sent my mama to the woodshed to collect spiderwebs—the older folk in those days, and black folks, mostly, used them as compresses to keep poison out of open wounds—and he set about making a cast for the hand with the only substance he knew to work.

"He rebuilt it with steel and a knowledge of anatomy he didn't have. It's ugly as the devil's own handiwork, I agree, I know that, but I can flex the fingers, I can hold the Book, I can lift up again what I have let go. It was a marriage of the human and the divine, a link of causation in the plan that leads to the glory of God." He looked out from behind it shyly.

The preacher stepped down to get closer to his audience, and he turned the couple as he went so that they faced the congregation too. Luce under his hand got corkscrewed awkwardly in her gown and began to tip, so Joseph had to grip her by an elbow to keep her vertical.

"Black folks out there, I would've got an *amen* or a *hallelujah* by now. Can I have one, please?"

An embarrassed momentary silence was broken by Parker, who raised his hand like a schoolboy. "Hallelujah," he said, grinning not at The Rev Roy but at Joseph.

"Amen, and thank you, sir. Listen to the Father when he says where not to be. Sin will make you dead or damaged. *This world is full of horses.*"

The Rev Roy smiled, waiting through the beginning of applause. "What's that story have to do with marrying? Just this: a marriage is a *marriage*, a joining of opposites, of man and woman, of iron and flesh, of God and man, of the unknown and the known. It won't always be pretty, but if you're faithful and you listen and you keep an open heart, it will last. It will *work*." He held up that damaged hand as proof.

He turned his back on the congregation then but left the young couple facing them, and finished the service. "Will you, Luce, cleave unto Joseph Taft? Love him no matter what? Forgive him anything and stay by his side, as long as you live?"

She tried to answer but had no voice. She nodded so vehemently that the audience laughed and applauded again.

"And will you, Joseph," The Rev Roy said, "*cleave* unto Luce Sears?" It came out cleeeeeeve, rising. "Cleave, I say. Love her no matter what, son? *Not run from her?* Forgive her anything and stay by her side, as long as you're alive?"

He nodded, and nodding let all the stored breath out in a hiss, an indefinite but definite *"Yesss,"* his first word ever, and his last.

Only Luce and The Rev Roy and those in the first pew heard him. The Rev Roy lifted his head and shouted. The miracle of tongues. His mother began to sob so loudly it silenced the roar of blood in his ears.

"Kiss each other, children. And praise God, you wedding guests, and welcome into the family of man Mr. and Mrs. Joseph Taft."

After the reception, Luce, shining, insisted on riding in the back of the pickup in her wedding gown, so he had to unfold and spread the blanket he still kept behind the seat. She tilted dangerously, precariously, on her heels and sat down with a thump when he eased the truck into gear. Like a beauty queen on a parade float, she pulled her bouquet apart flower by flower and let the petals fall like breadcrumbs as Joseph carefully drove her the two blocks from her parents' house into the swamp.

He lifted her, imagining he could feel the woman somewhere under the dozens of yards of bone-white satin wedding dress that threatened to smother him, and he carried her through the doorway he'd completed the day before, her feet just swinging clear of the threshold he'd fitted like a puzzle piece without nails, her head just missing the lintel he'd raised with his own hands.

I have a troubled cloudy vision of lands beyond,
which I cannot make out

Montaigne, "On Educating Children"

Side by side tombstones rise from dirt-hard plots in low, flattened oblongs and upright granite squares to lean against each other so closely the bodies underneath must crawl and hump and seethe. A catastrophe has happened—a starvation or plague; an extinction, anyway, on some huge scale—but it's a dream. Night after night for a month Joseph has risen from the bed he shares with Luce and walked to relieve his nightmares.

A cold front settled in the week before, smothering the Carolinas. It slipped this way and that, but not away, and a rime like damp ice began to coat the hickories and cypresses and sycamores. The swamp's ghostliness, he thought, probably added to the nature of his dreams.

His father is their engine. The signs of illness that Joseph had seen years ago, the discoloration in his father's face, are not yet here, but his hair is thinning and The Rev Roy's hair is almost white, so he has nearly caught up to that time.

He stood in workgloves and a holed sweater and jeans in the swamp at three in the morning, fifty yards from the house. The tin roof popped and pinged in the cold. A comma of smoke from the woodstove hung above the vent pipe. It looked like aluminum in the moonlight, like a machine's last breath.

Sometime soon (tomorrow, he thought, as the woodpile was nearly depleted from five days of fires) Luce would come to the door, call his name, and tell him to bring the wood. He'd raise that ax to answer her. That memory had stuck, and because it had he accepted its warning. He'd never gone back to the golf course, even though it was the northern border of his property, had never been hit between the eyes with the ball, had never sat up in the hospital room with the bandage corners brushing his eyelashes. He'd never been the Witch's pupil, never had to suffer her humiliations, although that had surely been close. He'd be careful with the ax tomorrow, or whenever, until that moment passed.

A bass leaped in the pond that drained the golf course. The sudden gunshot slap of water startled him, as always. He beat his gloved hands together and, knowing he couldn't see it, looked for a glint of its metal surface through the trees.

Instead, that glint comes in headlights winking against glass. He hears its motor, its tires on the dirt road. Luce is in the kitchen, humming, and he straightens from a crouch inside his front door, slides a screwdriver blade-up into his back pocket, and spins the hasp hanging in the wood by the start of a screw. Why is he putting on a lock?

Joseph knows the car outside by its engine noise; he pushes the door open and goes to meet his dad. There is no denying Frank's illness now: his face is gray in places, his back bent, his breathing like the wet, ragged wind of a run-over dog. Joseph takes him by an elbow and brings him inside.

"Your brother's missing," his father says haltingly. "Run away."

Louis is six, Joseph thinks, then corrects the estimate because of the clues in his dreams and doubles it. He walks his father into the kitchen and reaches for the phone.

"Hi, Dad," Luce says.

"What are you doing?" Frank asks his son.

Joseph dials the emergency number and holds the receiver out to his father.

"I've already called them. It used to be when a teenager left home, nobody panicked for a day or two, but nowadays—well, they're out looking. I'd hoped he'd be here."

Joseph shakes his head and points. *You.* His father holds the phone but won't speak into it. Joseph taps on the counter to get Luce's attention, but he already has it: she can hear the operator's voice saying, impatiently, "Emergency?"

She takes the phone from Frank's shaking hand and says, "We need an ambulance," and gives directions.

His father's slower leaving the house than entering it. They have him in a sled on wheels, sitting up but strapped in, and he's complaining, telling them he doesn't need to go to a hospital, not to make such a fuss, and at the same time telling them to be careful of the jamb, the two steps down, the dirt and gravel out front. Joseph pats his pocket for keys; he'll follow in the pickup.

"I'll call your mother," Luce says, and Joseph waves okay. Just as he's shutting the door a little boy comes into the kitchen and stands beside the cupboards. He's five or six, Joseph thinks, towheaded, as Luce says she was at that age. His eyes are a startling blue. "Where's Daddy going?"

His heart wants to stop. His hands and legs want to reverse themselves, but can't. He has his attention on his father and closes the door, but sticking the ignition key into its slot and glancing at the mirror out of habit, Joseph thinks, *I have a son.*

The ER is noisy. The ambulance men unload Frank like furniture to get their sled back. Frank seems not to notice. He huddles in a plastic chair behind the privacy drapes, hugging himself the way shy, well-built young women do, and stares at the toe of his left shoe as if it were slowly moving.

Just when Joseph can't wait any longer, a doctor finally introduces himself and asks Frank's name. "Now, then, what's the trouble, eh?"

Frank, without looking up from his shoe, says, "I don't know."

"Hop up here on the table and let me have a look."

Joseph has to help him because he hasn't the strength for the climb.

"Now, let's see." He lifts Frank's shirt carefully, as if it might be stuck to burned skin, and pokes, without looking, into a spot that makes his father jump. "That hurt? Of course it did. Sorry. Lie down. Loosen your pants. No, that's all right, keep your knees up if you need to." He pulls the curtain all the way around.

Joseph, drawing the belt tight in order to let it go, winces when his father does.

The young doctor reaches in and tugs Frank's slacks down, then the loose waistband of his undershorts. A scar Joseph doesn't know about reveals itself. It's scalloped, pink and white, and looks new.

"What's this?" the doctor asks for him. "Appendix?"

"Gallbladder," his father says.

"They should have put a zipper in," the doctor says. To Joseph he winks and asks, "How long has his color been like this?"

Five years, Joseph thinks, *plus however many more we are in the future from when I'm seeing this.*

"My son can't speak," Frank says. He shifts uncomfortably on the table, turning his nakedness away from Joseph. "I was a little green around the gills this morning."

Green's the only color not in your face.

"Bounce a quarter off your abdomen," the doctor says. "It's why I asked about the scar. I think you've got a bad appendix."

"That means an operation."

"Soon as I can get an OR running."

"Don't put me all the way under," Frank says. He grips Joseph's hand. "Don't let them."

"You can trust us, Mr. Taft."

"It's not that." He draws a noisy breath and waits until it settles in his lungs. "When they did the other one"—he points aimlessly, more at his son than his stomach—"I had a dream. I want to see if it's true." *I need to see if it's true,* his eyes say.

The doctor is speaking softly now to a nurse he's called. "What was it?" he asks Frank, not really listening. "The dream?"

"I heard the scalpel part my belly. Skin like a page tearing. Saw a cloud of green gas come up. Steam, I think, from me, under those green sheets and all that candle-power. Felt the nurse's fingers on my collarbone. Smelled oranges."

"Um, hmm." The doctor is done now with instructions and turns back to his patient.

"My God," Frank says, gasping. "It was the most . . . beautiful . . . moment of my life."

"Let's get going."

Two older men come in and wheel his father out. He raises a hand above one of their shoulders, a drowning man, and spreads two fingers. *Victory,* Joseph figures. *Going down for the second time. Peace.* If he hadn't held them apart, it could have been a blessing.

He follows as far as they will let him, to a pair of swinging doors, mills around in the hallway for a moment, then goes back and outside and paces some more in the parking lot until Luce and his mother arrive.

"What is it?" his mother asks. "Where is he?"

Joseph points to where his appendix must be, makes a fist, and yanks.

"The appendix?"

He nods.

"That's an easy one." With her eyes Helen asks Joseph, *Isn't it?*

He answers with his shoulders.

Every half hour in the waiting room makes Joseph's fingers drum harder on the chair, his feet tattoo the floor, and even the muscles in his back begin to spasm and flutter until he thinks he must look like a landed fish.

His mother smiles and, without raising her hands from her lap, points at a young man sitting at the end of the long line of chairs who is jitterbugging too. His eyes are closed; he's wearing headphones.

When's the last time he'd seen her smile? He pulls her from the chair by her elbows and holds her the way she'd held him when he was a child, then hugged himself in the cold. A muscle spasmed in his shoulder, and he windmilled his arm to loosen it. That same curl of smoke spiraled against the roof like a shoot of ghostly ivy. A bass leaped again, or maybe it was still the first time, and he walked back through the cold toward the house and his wife.

Here in this room that pink wallpaper he'd seen before looked silver now, and here was the woman he'd woken next to when Louise was still alive, and he could still remember how he'd felt: that she was a stranger to him, but not he to her. He stood at the foot of the bed and watched her sleeping, saw without any effort at all his own horizontal shape next to hers as if he weren't the one watching.

Luce lay half in and half out of the covers, one long bare leg shining in the heat of the house and in the reflection of that eerie outside light. Even he, with his long, twisted history, couldn't help but think that the things we're vulnerable to are unimaginable.

He got into bed, but not quietly, bumping against her and wanting her to wake, which she did, wanting to make love, which they did, hoping to make the son he'd seen briefly. He breathed in the warm, almost sticky smell of her as if it were that and not oxygen that he needed. This time it was Joseph who could have told Luce that she was pregnant.

Parker & Son worked short hours that week, starting late most days and even quitting at noon on Wednesday, partly because of the weather and partly because the job was winding down, so the super was trying to finesse the end-of-the-month budget. That was fine with Joseph; it gave him rare breakfasts together with Luce, and in the afternoons, when it warmed a little, he split wood for the stove in a growing pile.

He'd almost sliced through his cheekbone when Luce called for the wood. Everything in the memory played itself out: the cold front as it moved away left the Carolinas under a soft surprise snowfall, and Luce stood at the door against a warm, square halo of light, calling to him, and he raised the ax to say he'd heard her, and his hand slick in the glove with perspiration and the glove slick with the snow and the hard wood of the handle slick with cold all slipped at the same time, but a part of him was ready for it and he dodged the millimeter he needed to in order to save his carotid. He nicked an ear instead.

So he was home early on a Friday he wouldn't otherwise have had off with the ax in his hand when Higgerby stopped by. Joseph hefted it, letting the handle slide a bit, choking down to get a longer arc in the swing, and then let it slide further until his hand was at the butt and the blade was on the ground. The sweat on his forehead in a film he wiped dry with his sleeve.

Higgerby took forever picking his way across the yard to say hello. "It's warming finally," he said.

Joseph had to agree. He was splitting wood now for the pleasure of it.

"I didn't think you'd be here."

No? Come to see my wife?

"I was going to leave a message with Luce, or tack a note to your door and sneak over to the golf-course pond and wrestle a fish or two out of it until you got home. But here you are."

Joseph made a drinking motion and pointed to the house.

"I could put away a beer, I guess."

I could too.

Luce made Higgerby welcome, as she liked him quite a lot—more, Joseph thought, than he. She poured his beer into a glass and put a coaster under it, then handed Joseph his in a bottle.

"You're the first guest on the new couch," she said, almost pushing him down into it. "Tell me what you think."

"It's nice," Higgerby said. "Pretty."

"I know it's pretty," Luce said. "How does it sit?"

"It sits just fine."

"You mean it? It fits me, but Joe can't seem to be still in it."

Higgerby rested his arms on the back, then on the armrests, then crossed his legs, sat up, slouched. "No, it sits fine."

"Good. How about something to eat?"

"I'm going to catch dinner, thanks."

Leave him alone, Joseph wanted to say. *Let's hear what he's come for.* He unbuttoned the top of his workshirt and drank his beer.

Higgerby admired the couch some more—"Good springs, nice fabric"—and the new curtains Luce had put up in the kitchen window that Joseph hadn't noticed yet, and finished what was in his glass before he turned to Joseph. "Do you remember those pictures I took of your brain a long time ago?"

Joseph nodded.

"This fellow I've been working on—that screamer?—has something similar going on. Unusual activity in the parietal lobe. Left hemisphere."

Something similar. But one of us got constant noise and one of us got silence.

Higgerby was thinking along the same lines. "Same cause, I think, manifesting itself differently."

"Screamer?" Luce asked.

Joseph raised his hands—*It's impossible to explain*—and nodded when she turned to Higgerby and Higgerby looked at Joseph first.

"A patient I had a while back who couldn't stop yelling."

Both of them watched Luce trying to work out how—and when—Joseph had been involved. Joseph thought she connected it to her own tragedy, because she didn't ask any more questions.

"He's rational again."

Rational.

"He said something finally. Stopped screaming, I mean, and spoke. Weeks and weeks ago now."

Joseph waited.

"He said the sky was falling. Then the episode passed. It was over. A one-time thing, he hopes. It came on him when he was doing too much, overworked, 'like a freight train,' he said. 'All this future barreling down the tracks.'" Higgerby shook his head, mystified. "Said he never knew he was screaming. He wondered why his throat was so raw. He has damaged his vocal cords, in fact. He wasn't here but *there*, I guess, if that makes sense."

Joseph nodded.

Higgerby tried to shift his weight, but the couch had swallowed him. "Is that something you'd agree with? The sky falling?"

Joseph had to nod again.

"How do we go about paying attention to something like that? What do we do?"

There's a question, Joseph thought. He shrugged, thought some more about it, and shrugged again. Do nothing.

"The brain scans haven't offered up any help yet. Can't make much sense of them other than where the activity occurs." Higgerby tapped his head. "But I'm hoping somebody else can. I've been hunting around in the computer, sending out letters—SOS's, really. I'll let you know, of course, if I learn anything."

This time Joseph left the shrug in his eyes.

"Well." Higgerby slapped his thighs, and with his hands still in their imprints levered himself up. "I guess that's all I came for."

It was clear it wasn't, but when another invitation didn't come, he allowed Joseph and Luce to walk him to his car. Instead of getting in and driving off, Higgerby opened the trunk lid. He stared for a minute at his fishing tackle, the spare tire, a box of road flares. "I'm going to call it the Cassandra Syndrome," he said. "Do you remember who she was?"

Joseph shook his head, but Luce slipped an arm through her husband's. "She saw the future," Luce said, "but nobody listened."

Higgerby touched the side of his nose and winked. He lifted his pole and tackle box from the trunk, waved, and went looking for bass.

"Why don't you go with him?" Luce asked when he was out of sight and earshot. "I think he wanted you to."

He pretended to consider it for a moment, knowing he wouldn't, now or ever. Bass was the second thing Higgerby was fishing for.

Luce was pregnant again, although she refused to say that word. *With child,* she called her condition, using either Margaret's language or an incantation of her own devising that would protect mother and baby—he didn't know which. She had reached over in bed a month ago and cupped a hand around his ear, an unconscious gesture she had used, when they were younger, to impart special information. "I am with child," she'd said. "And I'm keeping this one." He'd sat up and nodded, holding his hands against both her ears in return, smiling so broadly that she knew without having to ask, "You've seen her?" and he'd answered—again, unnecessarily—that he had. He didn't tell her that their baby was a boy this time, but he did wonder how she kept getting it wrong.

"Is she beautiful?"

Handsome, Luce. Like my dad.

She flicked the light on, a dim bulb under a dark shade. "I worry about you being a father, you know. All the time. And I wonder too."

Wonder about what?

"Is it easier, or harder, or what?"

Easy?

"You get to see her skinned knees and bloody nose before she does."

What do you think, Luce? That I get to see everything? All of it? Who—including God—could stay sane through that? He shook his head, trying to tell her he didn't, that he lived only odd moments for no purpose. He thought of the fit he'd had, if that's what it was, and the picture of the hairy hand at the funeral reaching for the butter knife, and wondered again if the secrets weren't secrets but lies, or gossip from some unimaginable place. Small talk. He felt again as if he'd been invited to the wrong party, didn't know any of the guests. He gripped her hands and shut his eyes. I'm blind this time.

"I'll bet."

Luce started wearing elastic-waisted clothes before she needed to, and walking with her back arched. When she started collecting things—toys and clothes and diaper bags—she'd hold up two of an item (pajamas, for instance, on tiny hangers no larger than his hand), one pink, one blue. Without looking at him, she would weigh them, blue or pink tipping invisible scales in her mind, hoping, Joseph thought, that he would flash her a sign of some sort. He never did. But once, when she fingered and stared for far too long at a frock so frilly it could never in this century have been put on a son, he'd moved down an aisle of clothes for older children until he found in a nylon jacket the neon smear of color that he wanted, and lifted its sleeve and waved it until she noticed. *Lavender.* Whether she understood his whole meaning or not, she quit coyly asking him for hints.

She grew into her clothes and her walk soon enough. As she got larger and happier, Joseph seemed to shrink inside; the day's carryover, he thought grumpily, of balancing all night on the bed's edge.

"You're dreaming again, aren't you?" she asked him one morning before light.

He was staring into the coffee she'd put in front of him, counting the oily rings in it and thinking that this lack of sleep wouldn't be so bad except that he had to maneuver twenty tons of steel and rock for a living.

He shook his head, but she didn't believe him.

"It's not your dad again?"

He kept shaking his head, still answering the first question as well as the second.

"It's the baby, isn't it?"

Oh, no, honey.

But whatever look he had on his face—just tiredness, as far as he knew, or perhaps crankiness—set her new worry like a stain. She came up behind him and trapped his hands on the counter with her own. The hugeness of their son pressed into the small of his back.

"Tell me right now, Joe. What do you see?"

Except for that one brief glance of a little boy as he followed, or will follow, his father to the hospital, he'd seen nothing. While that made him ache, he didn't worry. Margaret had told the two of them that everything was fine, and Joseph had no reason not to believe her.

Another headshake wouldn't go very far. He pried her hands loose and swiveled on the bar stool, changing hands in a crossover as if he were square dancing or wrestling until he held hers, now, in his lap. He squeezed them, lifted them to his ears and then hers, and shook his head firmly. Nothing's wrong. *Everything's perfect.*

Luce let him go to work because she had to, but she stood in the door against the kitchen's light and watched him without waving. He backed the truck and flicked the high beams at her and turned and drove out, all the while thinking that he had to find a way to set her mind at rest. It reminded him of the fear he'd seen in his father's eyes long before there'd been any reason for it, and now, when health troubles of some grave nature were approaching, his father was oblivious to them. *The secret to living,* Joseph thought, *is to worry about only the right things.* He came to the end of the dirt and let the truck idle for a moment before he turned onto wet pavement. *Then again, I'm the only one who knows what those are, and it sure as hell has never done anybody I know any good.*

Parker & Son was helping build still another golf course. These hollows and hills were the skeleton of a body he'd never gone back to look at with its flesh on. He thought perhaps he ought to. Like the manhole lid he remembered lying on top of all that buried pipe in the middle of a road that wasn't a road yet, it would be nice to see the finish of things once and know what he'd had a hand in making.

Take your own advice, he thought a couple of hours later. He had the Diamond Reo in a precarious spot: its front wheels in sand, the truck on enough of a side slope to scare him, and all the weight in the bed—pit run—shifted so it wanted to crab. *Worry about the right things: all that soil with rocks you're carrying.*

He turned the wheels right, but not hard, against the slope, and eased the transmission into reverse. His hands were slick on the shift, the steering wheel, and the muscles in his thigh began to jump with his foot's pressure against the clutch. *Ease it up. Gently, gently. Come on, baby.*

It moved the way he hoped it would for about ten feet, then bogged down, the left wheel digging a hole in the slope so suddenly that he put the binders on, which sank the front end further. He should have straightened the wheel and given it more gas, more horses, but he couldn't now. A rock banged into steel behind him and sounded as if it were coming into the cab.

Then the Diamond Reo was moving like the start of an avalanche. He had two choices—jump or steer—and he sorted them quickly. Jumping could put him under the truck. Once he chose to steer it, he had to straighten the wheels or flip it. Joseph saw the picture in his head if he got it wrong (or even if he got it right but it was too late): the dump truck tilting a degree or two more and rolling, its load burying him alive if the cab didn't collapse around him first and crush him.

I've been here before; this'll be the second one I've ruined. Parker would have to fire him this time, new baby on the way or not. But the Diamond Reo, all its weight forward, skied a few feet, then dug in and stopped. Some of the load spilled over and cascaded down the windshield, one skull-sized rock starring it before denting the hood and rattling away. He waited until everything sliding on top and underneath him had stopped, then took the truck out of gear and, after another minute, turned the engine off. Like an idiot, he set the emergency brake before climbing out.

If he had chosen this spot to come back to years later, he would have found a short par 3 over water, the ground he was standing on now the middle of a pond.

Joseph dug the rest of the load out with a shovel, which took all day, and he had to listen to the guy whose shovel it was stand beside the truck and shout advice the whole time: "Use your legs, use your shoulders, your big muscles; use it like a broom; use it like a paddle," and then a catskinner winched the truck up onto the road with his bulldozer, and Parker drove it back to the yard, as silent as Joseph sitting beside him, his ear trained on engine and drive-train noises he didn't like.

And to make everything worse, it was payday. When Parker got into his pickup that night and pulled the checkbook from the glove compartment to write out Joseph's check, Joseph thought it would be his last one. In the six hours he'd spent with a shovel, the boss hadn't said anything. Parker signed it, blew on his signature and looked at it, and then handed it over through the open door.

"You okay?"

Me?

"Must've been a rough ride."

He lowered his head and with the hand that held the money touched his heart. I'm sorry.

"What happened?"

Joseph shrugged.

When he realized nothing else was coming, Parker said, "Goddamnit, you have to do better than that."

Joseph didn't blame Parker for his growing anger but honestly didn't know what to say. He hadn't been paying attention. He was tired. He'd had Luce on his mind. He'd even had, for God's sake, *golf courses* on his mind. He lifted his head and met Parker's glare. He meant to smile, but maybe he forgot. He touched his heart again, and then, with his hand in the air, waved the check. He meant it to mean, *There's lots of reasons for what happened, but I know none of them are any good; I've got no excuses worth listening to; thanks for the money and the job and not reaming me out,* but he couldn't think straight enough to make himself clear.

Parker misunderstood. "You're quitting?"

Joseph looked at the check he still waved like a white flag. Maybe he should give it back, for the windshield, for whatever else the accident would cost. He stuffed it into his pants before he could do something even more stupid.

You want me to?

Now both of them were confused.

Joseph saw Parker's knuckles rise as his hands tightened on the steering wheel. He reached for the key hanging in the ignition. "Sleep on it," he said, maybe to himself, and started the engine. "I'll talk to you on Monday."

Joseph watched Parker's truck slice through the dark with the same misgivings in his heart that Luce must have had that morning. What should he tell her, if anything? And how? The frustration his mother had never stopped letting him know about, *not knowing how he felt,* he felt now.

Luce had kept dinner waiting in the oven, and by the time he got home and showered and seated at the table, it was dry. She took a forkful of the casserole, made a face, and left her fork standing up in it. "It's not like you to be late," she said. "What's the matter?"

Had he ever had to answer so many questions, each with its own hidden trouble? He gave her a zero, the sign he used lately for *Nothing*.

But she could set her clock by the one on the job site, and Joseph never stayed around to drink with the others, and here he was two hours late, so she asked once again, "What is it?"

Normally she would have reached across the table to tap his hand or some such gesture—maybe lay her fingers on his forearm as softly as feathers so the emotional meaning was completely clear—but this time she sat looking from him to her fork and back again, waiting. *She's still brooding about this morning,* he thought. *Or maybe more than that; maybe she's angry by now.*

He put his fork down too, as she had, impaling the casserole, and closed his eyes and blew out a breath.

He tapped his watch.

"You're late."

He nodded, pleased. After all, it could have been the beginning of a long-winded reconstruction of some future event. He moved a steering wheel in his hands.

"Driving the truck. Does a *because* go in between the two?"

He nodded.

"You're late *because* you were driving the truck, *and?*"

He hit the palm of his hand with a fist.

"You crashed."

It was almost a pleasure for a moment to see her own words sink in. "You *crashed?*" Now she moved, levering herself out of the chair and hurrying around to hug him, and he had to stand to help her with it or she would have toppled over. As it was, she bumped the table and spilled the milk. He stroked her head. *It's all right.*

Luce was crying. "It's *not* all right. Are *you* all right?"

I'm fine.

I knew something was wrong with somebody, her look said. "Let me see."

She started with his hair, parting it in handfuls to look for wounds, then ran her hands down the sides of his face and his neck and under his collar as if she were blind, as if there might be holes she couldn't see. "Take off your shirt."

Come on, Luce.

"Take it off."

Grinning, partly out of embarrassment, he took it off.

"Turn around."

He struck a bodybuilder's pose—*like a crab,* he thought—and turned around for her. A new car in the showroom.

"Your pants."

He crossed his hands at his crotch, put his knees together, fluttered his eyelashes.

"Come on."

He shook his head.

She shook hers too. "Give it up, mister; you can't win this."

He unbuckled his belt, popped the fly buttons, and pulled his jeans off slowly, a leg at a time, his hand on her shoulder for balance. His arms from the middle of his biceps to his hands, and his neck and face, were tanned mahogany. The rest of him was so white he looked unhealthy.

"Your underwear," and then, to stop his protest, she said, "Oh, hell, I'll do it."

She left him standing like that, naked in the doorway to the kitchen, and stood back and studied him with her hand under her chin as if she were buying a painting. "Well, I guess you're not hurt."

I told you that.

"But I have to be sure. I should see if everything still works. You might have whiplash or something."

When she was undressed too, and he was helping her down onto the bed, he put a hand on the swell of her belly but left it there a moment too long.

She stiffened. "What is it?"

What's what?

"Our baby's not all right, is she? Tell me now."

Oh, Christ. You've got to let the fear go, Luce. He stared at her, trying to bore into her skull so his thoughts would fit there. He couldn't keep this up for the next month and a half. *Or for a lifetime,* he suddenly realized.

She confirmed that last fear: "*When's* the trouble, Joe? Count the years for me with your fingers."

It's all right.

Luce sat stiffly and awkwardly on the bed, naked, beautifully misshapen, like a fertility figure carved from yellow pine or some other warm, shiny wood, as vulnerable as any icon. He held out his two hands in front of her, all the fingers spread.

"Ten."

Again.

"Twenty. Thirty. Forty. *Fifty? Sixty? Seventy!*"

That ought to be enough.

But after they'd made love, carefully, following a picture in a pamphlet Margaret had given them, and he was drowsing, she snuggled against his chest. "Joe?"

He patted what had once been her waist. *What?*

"What is it that happens to her when she's seventy?"

On Sunday morning Joseph drove to the job site to see what damage he'd done. He unlocked the chain-link gate to the equipment yard, leaving it open, and pulled up beside Parker's two Diamond Reos. The one he'd wrecked was sitting beside the other, out of view, as if Parker wanted to hide it.

It looked worse than he remembered. The windshield the rock had starred was in fact buckled, sagging in the center of a galaxy of cracked glass. He might have been able to match the dent in the hood if he had stood on top of it and given it several blows with a twenty-pound sledge. The paint was already curling up around it. But that damage, though expensive, was cosmetic. He could see even before he stood behind to line it up that the dump bed was skewed on its hoist, and from the front, staring at the massive chromed grill, it was obvious that the cab was twisted on the frame. Worse yet, somehow—aesthetically, he supposed—the front and rear were torqued in opposite directions. He'd done something similar once to a toy truck, playing in the backyard.

He sighed and crawled underneath. A pinion gear was bent, which meant the rack would need replacing too. Maybe the axle. He'd begun brushing away the oil-caked sand to see what else was wrong when he heard Parker's truck.

He saw, from under this dump truck and the next one, the pickup's tires stop (so tiny next to these huge ones), saw Parker's boots drop into sight, saw them turn in a circle as Parker looked for him, then walk around to where he was.

"Joseph? You underneath?"

I have until tomorrow, he thought, but scuttled out anyway on his palms and shoe soles, then stood and faced his boss and brushed off the greasy sand.

"Pretty bad?"

Joseph nodded, put his hands in line one behind the other, fingers to heel, and twisted them.

"Yeah. Steering?"

Shot.

"Let's put the bed up, then, and see what's what. I should have done it yesterday."

Joseph pulled the tailgate pins and climbed up into the cab and started it. The engine sounded okay, and the engine, he hoped, was what mattered most.

Parker gave him a thumbs-up, then the whole hand.

The bed had hardly begun to move before it began squealing, and Joseph had it back down again before Parker could react.

"Well, that sounds like shit," Parker said.

Sounds like my voice. That's about right, too; God probably had something else on his mind when he should have been paying attention.

"Take it up again until I holler."

He gave the engine a little gas and hit the PTO, and the bed lifted, squealing. The truck bounced, its fourteen wheels chattering for a moment against the dirt. In the side mirror Joseph could see its list, could see Parker stick his head under it and follow the hydraulic cylinder, and then the greasy piston, with his hand.

"Hold it there."

Something lets go now, and Lonnie's an orphan. But Parker backed out again, held a fist up to say *Stay put,* and disappeared. He came back with an arm-length four-by-four and wedged it between the frame and the bed.

"Let it down easy."

The bed settled noisily onto the blocking, and Joseph heard the wood crack once, but apparently it was solid enough because Parker drew a finger across his throat. Joseph turned the engine off and got out.

Parker pointed: bent piston. "I don't see anything else wrong," he said. "If that's all there is, we're in good shape. Hell, I can fix that myself, we get the part Monday and a hoe to hold the bed up for an hour."

Joseph got back under the truck with Parker and pointed to the rack and pinion, then ran a finger along the axle.

"Axle's okay, I think. Both fenders're cracked, but that's fiberglass."

Joseph had missed that.

They wiggled out and Parker sat in his pickup and figured it on a scratchpad. "Couple thousand, counting the windshield but not the hood or fenders. Don't know if it's worth giving to the insurance."

Joseph banged a hand against the near truck. Count the hood and fenders.

"Oh, I'll do it all right, I just don't know how to figure the cost. It's always more than you think, that pretty stuff."

Joseph opened the passenger-side door and got in, moved a roll of plans aside, then popped the glove and pulled out Parker's checkbook.

"Yeah," Parker said slowly, "that's where it'll come from."

Joseph tore a check out, handed it to himself, ripped it in half. It's what he'd wanted to say Friday night but didn't know it.

"Take it out of your wages?"

Joseph nodded, then grinned awkwardly. He put his thumb and forefinger together. A little bit at a time.

Parker considered it, and Joseph. "Job-site accident," he said. "You might have paid with more than money."

I didn't, though. He tapped his skull with a forefinger and shook his head.

"Not broken?"

Not that. *Well, that too.* He shook it again.

"Weren't thinking?"

Yes.

"Your fault?"

Yes.

"Lot on your mind?"

Yes.

"How's Luce and the baby?"

The question caught him off guard, and Parker misread the pause.

"Everything's okay, isn't it?"

Not you too. He nodded, but he could see that Parker didn't completely believe him.

Parker looked down at his scratchpad for a long while, then tore the sheet off and put it in his pocket. "These things happen," he said. "It's a dangerous world.

Lots of horses under lots of hoods around here. Let it go." He turned the key, and Joseph got out. "See you Monday," he said. "Get enough sleep." Parker drove about a dozen feet and stopped, and put his head out the window. "And Joseph? Thanks."

Joseph watched him go, feeling guilty that it had worked out this way, that Parker had based his decision on a lie of sorts, a misunderstanding that Joseph had let ride, nothing short of pity, really, for an innocent baby and a pregnant wife, but he was relieved anyway. What did that make him besides a thief? And more: everything he'd ever stolen, he'd stolen from Parker, the best friend he had. And Parker had *thanked* him.

Higgerby's car was in front of the house when he got home. Joseph sat in the pickup, letting it run, thinking about turning the wheel one revolution and running himself. *This is too much.* He felt as crowded as his baby.

He was even more surprised to find Higgerby inside when he finally went in, sitting with Luce on the no longer brand-new furniture, a beer glass and two empty bottles beside him. Joseph had assumed without thinking that Higgerby had come to fish.

What's this?

"I called him, Joe."

What's wrong?

Higgerby struggled to stand up. "Luce thought—"

"Let me do this." Luce's hands lay on her belly, crossed and resting on it in the same fashion her feet were, propped up on the ottoman. "I thought Alan might know your mind."

About what?

"You know I'm having these awful dreams about the baby, and I can't help thinking you know something and won't say." Her hands tapped her belly nervously before she could still them. "I feel terribly alone in this." She pushed against the chair arms, and Joseph thought she was going to rise, but she only wanted to bring her feet down to massage a cramping thigh. "Almost as alone as the man—" She gestured and turned to Higgerby for help.

"The screamer."

"As he must have been," she said. "As you must sometimes be. I thought Alan might know something that would help."

About what? he thought again, but he knew about what. When had Luce ever not trusted him? Why did she think Higgerby could know anything about him that she didn't?

"It's Luce, mainly, who needs to talk," Higgerby said. *And,* he didn't have to say, *have someone talk back.*

Joseph turned all his questions on him.

"Well, I *am* a psychiatrist, Joseph."

You are?

At his look, Higgerby said, "Surely you knew that."

Joseph, thinking about what he did know, slowly shook his head. He'd tagged Higgerby as a brain doctor, somebody who did something technical with brain scans, the kind of doctor you'd call into an emergency room. The muted warnings he'd half heeded all these years now sounded clearly in his head.

Joseph sat now, heavily, leaving Higgerby standing alone. What about his life did he know for sure?

Higgerby caught the echo of Joseph's thought and turned it. "Luce just needs to know that no harm is coming to the baby. No harm that you know of, I mean."

Joseph sat for a long minute with his eyes closed, his fists and forearms and stomach clenched, then forced himself to relax and stand. He flicked a finger in a blur at his eye, his mouth, his wife. *I told you.* He left his hand up, helplessly. *You're worrying about a future that isn't true.* He pointed the same finger at Higgerby and then let it drop because he had no idea of what he wanted to say to him except, *I'd give you back your bicycle if I still had it.*

He walked out, leaving the door open, intending to go into the swamp, to sit and think, to hide, but at the last minute turned to the pickup instead and got in and started it up. Higgerby was around so damned often even the swamp didn't feel like his anymore.

"Joseph," Higgerby said from the door.

"Joe?" Luce asked from inside.

"Will you cleave to her, Joseph?" The Rev Roy asked from even further inside. "Love her no matter what? *Not run from her?*"

He backed the truck through a cloud and then spun in it and watched in the mirror as the dust and exhaust settled around his house, all of it—the whole day—glowing with late orange light. He braked for a 'possum ambling in front of him, who stopped and glared and bared his filed teeth, then accelerated through tree shadows and the warm rush of summer air vibrating with the wings of insects and the perfumes of growth and decay. Except for the road and the houses (and then he was past them), this could be the beginning of time.

The woods on either side were lit with fireflies. The cab too begins to flicker and glow, alive with those lightning bugs, and he knows this isn't a vision but another seizure and he is about to fall into a nightmare like the screamer's. He can't feel the pedal under his foot or the wheel in his hand, and the balance in his ear plummets like a barometer.

The sky fills with blossoms of fire that climb through the clouds for handholds like a vine of morning glory, but the clouds aren't clouds, they're smoke. He's in a crowd on a sidewalk up against a parking meter in a town he vaguely recognizes—it's slightly familiar but unknown, a feeling he's well used to—and the last arriving siren crawls down to a growl and airbrakes, *tcshh, tcshh, tcshh,* hiss on. A woman firefighter jumps from the cab and a man's hand grips her shoulder, tucks her blonde hair safely into her collar. The slither of hoses on pavement sounds like serpents shedding their skins. Half a brick wall crumbles dancing with sparks into the street, and the sudden heat sends the crowd milling backward. His shoe is stepped on.

"Sorry."

The air shimmers again, and at first he thinks it's another wave of heat, but it's another building, another fire. This one is a house, its chimneys falling in a smoking clatter like dominoes, its windows exploding, a decorative tree of some sort, a Japanese elm, he thinks, in the front yard dripping fire. A crowd swells here too, spilling onto someone's lawn. Moving under canvas overalls, that figure is familiar. In the crowd, watching both of them, is his brother, Louis.

More fireflies, but these are blinking in the air for real and not just behind his eyes: cinders, winking on and out like Christmas lights, dying as they land on his arms and his gloved hands. He holds an ax, and this panics him. The building he is running into is an apartment house, and he has to fight against a falling tide of families on the stairs. Against his back, a small palm pushes with enormous strength.

He sucks air through a mask from a bottle on his back like a deep-sea diver, like an astronaut, through the clean working bellows of his lungs without a whistle. He knows that when he climbs back down these stairs with that blonde firefighter over his shoulder, the hole in her air hose hissing, her butt in the crook of his elbow, her breasts against the shifting slabs of his shoulderblades, and kicks open the front door that has swung shut and swelled in the heat, and strides back to the street and the crowd and the cops and the photographers, he'll lay her on the pavement, perhaps, next to the pumper truck, unzip her overalls and open her collar, pull that sheaf of gold hair out, maybe unbutton her shirt, give her mouth-to-mouth.

His hands, though, are wrist-deep in gooey clay, and the form he's shaping isn't feminine, or male either. Not animal or mineral or vegetable. The objects in the world that he knows—the concrete physicality that he's lived in for twenty years—flutter past his vision like the glossy color pictures in the pages of an encyclopedia, arranged in the mind's alphabet, and this thing isn't any of them. It's horrific and insubstantial; it's God's other nature. He remembers art class, his art teacher, and has to restrain his hands as if they belong to someone else, has to will them into stillness, his ten fingers into silence, to keep from touching the figure the way an artist would, bringing it to life.

The clay on his fingers has dried to chalk. He steps away from a blackboard where equations stare back like hieroglyphs, their once-simple geometries now fused incorrectly. He has readied himself to answer a question from his teacher but can't get it off the tip of his tongue. *Solve for* Δv.

Light floods Joseph's desert places, and he pictures again as clearly as before that carpet of life's history, but this time, hovering above it, he sees that the threads are strings of colored sand arranged by the wind—*it's howling*—on a table of stone. In all directions lies dry and colorless desolation. Someone else is with him, behind him, which is above him, but he cannot force himself to turn; he doesn't know how to get a purchase in the air.

A spasm in his hand, a cramp, turned the wheel away from an oncoming truck that's crowded onto the opposite shoulder, its lights on high beam blinding him, its horn shrieking. It rushed past with just enough room. Joseph heard the air between their side mirrors tick; it was squeezed that close—just the knurl of one screw from shattering—and his imagination gave him the almost-happened future of glass shards filling the cab in a spray.

He drove another hundred yards coasting from inertia, the white line centered on his hood, then slewed off the highway at a sudden mirage in this empty place and into the gravel parking lot of a renovated barn, a neon-flickering topless dance joint. He stretched, feeling the miles go. He could see his heart pounding through the fabric of his shirt. *My mouth is full of blown and blowing sand.*

The tinny music made his flesh pucker and jump while he was still outside. The New South and its resulting tourism (those golf courses) had gutted all the old Sunday blue laws. Two-drink minimum; beers with brand names he didn't know were five dollars apiece. He took a table in a corner and ordered both of them.

The girls on stage hadn't grown into their shapes yet, were all colt-skinny legs and high, small breasts. Two or three of them moved to the music, but most didn't bother, just stood humping a pole like a horny dog would somebody's leg. A redhead, freckled everywhere, made a show of removing her transparent bra and G-string, but even that teasing was mechanical. The others walked onto the stage and into the light already naked, already bored, already glaring.

He felt like a pedophile and wanted to go, but at the same moment he told his muscles to stand two lit cages descended from the high, dark recesses of the barn's ceiling. The women—not girls—who were standing in them had bodies with curves just hidden under shimmering, feathery negligees, and almost against his will he stayed to watch.

They danced an old language of hips and hands and stomach grinds, of neck archings, of shoulder rollings, of thigh partings, their clasped hands vised between their knees in a prayer against fertility. Sometimes they pressed their fingertips or lips against the smudged plexiglass walls of their terrariums like mimes—as, he thought, he pressed against the glass of his own life—and Joseph couldn't help but see the black widow or centipede or june bug he'd kept in a mayonnaise jar as a kid. He'd punched holes in the lid with a screwdriver, but even with air the longest they'd lasted was a week.

When they finished, to whistles and hoots and shouting applause, when the cages had risen again to the ceiling and a catwalk that must be up there, Joseph finally got up to go out, to go home, but went to the men's room instead. His zipper was halfway down when the sound of its separating teeth, like raw fabric tearing, parts more than his jeans.

He rises in his mind from the azaleas out front on knees like springs, shading his eyes against the dark to stare through chintz curtains. A hand—his—drives a screwdriver between the sashes and levers the lock. One last glance over his shoulder before he slides the window up and steps through: that's his parents' house behind him.

Joseph stands like a ghost, pleased with how smoothly the machine can work. He can hear his blood hum. It feels as if he is standing on a thin layer of air, or on ice. Something warm and small moves against his ankle. The Allisenis' cat. He stoops, lifts, reaches, lets go, and the cat is outside, the window softly closed. *I'm made of water.*

Shapes solidify into lamps, tables, chairs. An ashtray, two bottles, a glass standing in a melt puddle on the coffee table. A magazine spread-eagled on the carpet. Flowers in a vase. He moves like liquid into the hall, then toward the master bedroom at the end. The door is open, and he stands in its arch for a moment, one foot inside, the other in the hall, giving the room's air time to accept him.

Mrs. Alliseni sprawls where she fell, half under the covers, half on top, half in her nightdress, half out, too asleep, too drunk, to listen to her skin's alarm. *I've known for years that I could do this if I wanted.*

He shakes his head, closes his eyes. Like a veil or a curtain lifted, or a cloud disintegrating, the chipped and graffittied men's room tile in front of him glows with messages. He sees in each piece, in the mosaic of color, form, and language that they make, a future he's been to, each piece pulsing like a pump, humming like neon, *breathing,* it seems, and then the wall dissolves in an intake of breath, an inspiration, the diamond-shaped tiles one at a time blowing or scattering or dripping away like the meaning he'd never been able to find in constellations. On the other side of what had been a wall, his wife and son are talking to each other with their hands. *He'll inherit this.* He takes a step—then two—toward them and the men's room door opened by itself into his hand, and he left the bathroom, where he'd been standing for who knew how long, and found the place was emptied, closing, the naked women dressed and gone. At the door he watched the sweeper, a black kid of about fifteen with a stiff broom his own height, sweep up the beer labels and matchbook covers and cigarette butts from the sticky floor. Joseph's last image of the place was that kid standing in one of the cages, the puff of his broom lifting the sequins that had dropped from the girls' costumes, turning them in the air like dust motes.

Choosing west wasn't enough to get him home, as he had no idea where he was and with the light gone didn't know which way west was in any case. He followed other taillights (the driver of that car in his headlights was a blonde) so he wouldn't have to think, wouldn't have to make another decision, and when they finally crossed a larger road he swung onto it and went twenty-five miles in the wrong direction before realizing it was south he wanted. He was half an hour into another state.

The lights and bridges of his own town finally swam up in the windshield, feeling like another of those future dislocations, but he'd driven here. He let the truck idle, looked at the gauges: *Gas is low, nearly gone.* He coasted down his old street, a block from his parents' house and the Allisenis', almost home from a night he shouldn't have spent away. His head hurt from driving. His groin swelled with desires raised but not relieved. His heart was sore with the same thing.

His parents' house looked dark and safe. A cricket called loudly over his engine's noise. The Sears house, though, was lit, and Luce's car was in the drive.

His truck slipped past three more houses while he was deciding whether to stop, and he wound up circling the block before parking the pickup half in the street behind her car. He got out carrying his headache like somebody else's suitcase, rang the bell, waited, then rang it again. Luke Sears opened it but didn't move aside, so he and Joseph filled the open door, blocking each other's way. His father-in-law's cane tapped twice on the welcome mat, as if leading a blind man, and came to rest between them. "Thought it might be you," Sears said.

Joseph was too tired for conversation, and anyway this was the kind of moment that didn't need words.

"Come on in. You smell like beer."

Luce's mother and Luce and her younger sister Gail were sitting in the living room, the chair where Luke had sat still with the dent of him in it. Hopscotch, an old setter, thumped his tail hello three times but didn't get up.

Joseph looked in their eyes for signs of a jury and relaxed a bit when he didn't find them. Luce waved her fingertips without lifting her hands from her lap.

"Hello, Joseph," Linda said.

Gail said, "You look like hell."

And I feel it. He smiled at Luce's sister, nodding, then her mother, then thought the beer smell might escape so clamped his lips shut. Too late; Gail's nose was wrinkling like a rabbit's. He tapped his watch and gestured almost imperceptibly with his head: *Can we go?*

"I guess we should." Luce heaved herself up with Gail's help. She pinned Joseph with a look: *Where have you been?*

"Stay if you want." Luke had come up behind Joseph, pretty quietly for a cane-stumper. Carpets.

We don't live a quarter-mile from here.

Luce took his hand, giving it an extra squeeze, but whether it was anger or reassurance he didn't know. "I'm talked out," she said, dropping Joseph's hand and stretching to kiss her father's cheek. "But thanks."

Luke barred Joseph's way as the women walked, still talking, toward the door. "Luce is scared," he said quietly. "Has she anything to be scared about?"

Joseph's lazy nod to the first part turned into an emphatic headshake.

"You know she's worried?"

Everybody in the world has told me that. *What makes him think she wouldn't?*

"But you run off anyway, all night, and leave her alone?"

Joseph caught his anger before it rose all the way, like a good shortstop, and considered his father-in-law. *He has two more daughters at home,* Joseph reminded himself, *which makes him take all this very seriously. Perhaps that's unfair; perhaps he's worried because Luce is worried, and nothing else, and now she's worried doubly because I've been gone half the night.*

Luke mistook Joseph's look of contrition. He put a fatherly hand on his shoulder. "Okay," he said. "No doubt the two of you will work it out."

At home, Joseph helped Luce from her car and walked her to the door, but when he reached around her to open it she began beating on his chest with her fists.

"Where the *hell* have you been?"

Where hadn't he? He hung his arm out a window, gripped a wheel. Driving around.

"Go on, tell me. Tell me!"

Looking in my own windows. I'd tell you if I could, Luce.

She blocked his way to the bedroom, her hands in front of her as if she were going to raise them for punching. He lifted his own to talk and realized, shocked, when hers came up too, that she was ready to ward off his touch.

"It's nearly three o'clock. I can smell the beer and smoke and perfume. The beer and smoke I can figure out for myself." With a forefinger she tapped her belly like a watermelon, then rested both palms on its curve. "There's no room for any more women in your life, Joe."

It should be easier to be honest or untruthful—either one—when you can't speak, but he found himself unable to answer her accusation with even a coherent thought. He held up his left hand, waving his wedding ring in her face, careful to keep the fingers harmlessly spread. Then he too tapped her belly with a finger. He pointed at his watch, at the bedroom, and then at the front door, made the driving motion that always meant *Work* or *Parker,* and turned before she could stop him. He slammed the door behind him so hard the roof shook.

She swept something from the kitchen counter that bounced and broke, opened the door, and wailed, "Are you going to leave me *again?*"

Her last word rang like an echo—*again, again, again*—and slowed his foot. Joseph finished the step he started but couldn't start another. He stood that way for a long minute thinking of nothing, then shrank until he was sitting cross-legged—his back still to her—in the dirt halfway between the house and his truck. A weight grew in his spine and he leaned forward until his forehead and elbows were on the ground, then rolled onto his side.

"Joe?"

That word was low, rumbly, as if it had traveled an enormous distance.

When she'd lumbered over and, grunting, knelt, she found his face wet, his eyes closed but his eyelids jumping, his hands as loose-jointed as a cadaver's.

"Joe?"

Luce tried to lift his arm, thinking to drag him upright so he'd have to face her, have this out, breathe better, whatever, but she needed two hands and still couldn't do it. His bicep might as well have been made of iron. "You're scaring me. Joe? *Joe!*"

Joseph hadn't gone anywhere; he felt her too-warm hands on his arm, felt the frantic tugs, heard her panic, and wanted to open his mouth to say, *I'm all right, just let me rest for a minute.* He wanted to open his eyes, but that was too much, so he thought he'd just open one of them, the right one, the one nearest Luce. He formed the command for that but couldn't send it. In the center of his brain was a small red switch he didn't have the strength to turn.

"I'm calling Alan," she said. "Or an ambulance, or both."

Call an electrician, Joseph thought. *I've fried a fuse.*

The ambulance arrived first. Two men had him by his knees and elbows, as rigid as a turtle, trying to tip him a couple of inches so they could slide the sled under, when he felt Higgerby's hurried steps. *The earth's a drum.*

"Hey, Doc, this guy's heavy. What causes that?"

Higgerby laid a hand on Joseph's neck. "What do you mean, what causes that?"

"I mean he's *heavy*. The two of us can't lift him. We'd lift you easier."

"Nonsense."

"I ain't kiddin', Doc. Ever pick up a tomcat that wants to fight? Got his center of gravity so low it's like pickin' up a sack of cement? This is like that, but worse. Goin' to take an engine hoist."

"He goes one-eighty, one-ninety," Higgerby said. "No more than that."

"Shit, Doc, I've lifted fat dead people twice his size. Go ahead, try and lift an arm."

He felt Higgerby's hand on his wrist. *Like an insect on a root.*

"I'll be damned," Higgerby said. And then after a long minute, "Call another crew to help."

Even with four men and Higgerby they could lift him only far enough to slide the sled under; they couldn't lift it after.

"Engine hoist," one of them said again.

"Forklift."

"He's a man," Higgerby said, "not an I-beam."

Velocity increases mass.

"Oh, yeah?"

The radios in the ambulances crackled in stereo. "What ya wan' do, Doc?"

"Leave him here," he heard Luce say.

"What? You can't, Luce."

But Higgerby didn't know that tone the way Joseph did.

"Can't?" Luce asked. "Can't do anything else, you mean. He's breathing okay, isn't he? His heart's all right?"

"His vitals are good," another voice said.

"I don't think Joe's going anywhere," Luce said. "I'll sit with him. Give me your beeper number in case anything changes."

"Catalepsy can last years, Luce. A lifetime."

She put a hand in her husband's hair. "No. He's got a little girl to meet next month."

The argument shifted back and forth, but she won, as he knew she would. When everybody finally drove off, she covered him with the blanket he still kept behind the seat in the pickup. At the end of the day she brought out the sofa cushions and lay down beside him. "It's growing light now, Joe," she said. "The cedars are blue."

He sees Luce as he had the first time: sliced from the edge of sight, standing inside her home on the other side of the sliding glass door to the pool, and as he had the second time: blurred by her family, by the water running over his eyes and the knowledge inside them, from the feet up, knees and waist and chest and chin and all that gold hair lit from behind. It's the same image, one on top of the other, and he adds another and still another, like the faces of playing cards painted on glass, stacked into a deck that he holds in his mind's hand: Luce with her arm raised, calling from the door, Luce laughing, her head back, the cords in her neck like braided rope, Luce undressing, Luce unobserved, older by decades, deep in the swamp where she says she never goes and sitting as still as the heron she's watching, Luce coy, Luce clumsy, and both at once, Luce sweating over her garden, the tops of her shoulders red, Luce at Christmas, so bright she's an ornament, Luce, lovely Luce. Luce with *children*.

When Joseph opened his eyes in the middle of the afternoon, Luce was sitting next to him on the ottoman she'd brought from the house. *A couple of human stones in the yard,* he thought. He sat up and smiled.

"You've got an interesting way of avoiding fights," she said, and kissed him. "But it's not over. We'll finish it when you're better."

We can finish it anytime you like, Luce. The hurry is over.

But not for her. She delivered ten days early, on the fifth of July, a day so hot even the unpaved job site shimmered like a dream. Level roads in that heat looked rutted, washboarded, and even though he knew they weren't, his arms and legs tired from tensing for dips that weren't there. His father, driving far too fast, enveloped in a dust cloud, swerved into the path of his Diamond Reo like the end of a chase scene in a television movie, flashing the headlights, honking and banging on the car's roof with the flat of his hand. That told Joseph it was Luce. His father's smile through the dirty windshield told him she was all right. He set the brake *and* turned the truck's engine off *and* left it in gear, his father had stopped so close to the bumper.

"It's Luce," his dad said. "She's in labor. Come on."

Joseph, standing on the Diamond Reo's running board, nodded, then pointed to the dump bed. This load.

"Come now."

Five more minutes, Dad, will be all right. Move your car.

It took a minute to make his father understand, or agree, and Frank followed the dump truck so closely that

Joseph had to get out again when they stopped and point his father away from the place he had parked, where Joseph needed to back up. Then he had to track Parker down to tell him.

"Go," Parker said. "Tell Luce I'm thinking of her."

His father drove like a maniac, pushing the heat in front of them like a horizon. Twice Joseph had to point to his eye and then to the windshield. The second time—*Watch the road, damn it*—so forcefully that his father actually did.

He heard Luce shouting while he was still in the hospital corridor, but the room he walked into wasn't the one he'd seen, wasn't the one he'd visited in the future that was now, hadn't been made to look like a bedroom, and so he was confused. Frank—Grandpa—was gently pushed back out, but Joseph was allowed to remain.

"Father's here," Margaret said, and winked.

He felt like waving, would have, perhaps, had Luce not been screaming.

"Your job is to hold your wife's hand and tell her she's the bravest creature on earth, and otherwise stay out of the way."

Yes, ma'am.

"This baby is racing." To his worried look, she said, "I just mean it's in a hurry. Good for everybody."

Luce had just bitten down on a wad of sheet, the tears leaking into her ears from the wrong corners of her eyes. Joseph saw the pain in them stop just like that, the tension go in a slackening of her jaw and face, and he looked up at the doctor in time to see her lift the baby from between his wife's legs.

Goo and hair, but between the baby's legs no dangle. *Where is it? What's gone wrong?*

Margaret's eyes glittered behind her mask. "Luce, honey, you have a beautiful daughter."

Daughter. He heard a little boy saying, *Where's Daddy going?* and the hollow thunk of a door slamming a long way away. *Is she having twins? Does his son have an older sister?* Impossible. He'd been there.

Bright lights tipped into his eyes. "He'll . . . be . . . ohh . . . kay," he could hear Margaret say. "It . . . hap . . . pens . . . to . . . lots . . . of . . . new . . . fah-ah-ah . . . thers."

He felt lighter when he sat up: not light-headed but physically less dense, as if a debt his body owed were gone. When he stood, an unnamed part of him inside shifted, settling back to the earth with a thump that was nearly audible.

Joseph, not Luce, was the one in Recovery, on a cushioned table. A cold cloth fell from his eyes when he sat up. A nurse peeled it off his lap at his movement and gave him a look she reserved, he guessed, for cowardly husbands.

She couldn't know, though, that it *was* cowardice: it would be so much safer in so many ways to have a son.

"Luce and Sarah Kay would like to see you, when you've got a minute. That's your wife and daughter, if you're still groggy."

He heard, *Don't blame the horse.*

A son hadn't followed Sarah Kay, then or later. For a year or two, at odd, mindless moments, the thought would slide into his head: *She'll tell me any minute that she's pregnant with our son,* but Luce never did. The absence of the boy who had never been grew almost as real to him as the absence of his sister, so much so that he grieved, and packed his grief away the best he could as a guilt he wouldn't even name, just another of the futures that couldn't be.

But even he couldn't hide those feelings in a place Luce couldn't find them, though it looked to her like something it wasn't. To her it seemed as if Sarah Kay were a painful reminder to her husband—particularly now, as she was six—a living memory of his childhood horrors, not the joy she was meant to be, and was, to her mother. The old worry about what he might have seen had never left her.

"You're more silent than ever," she said to him at breakfast.

He smiled quizzically to tell her that wasn't possible.

"I mean it."

She gave him hotcakes and bacon, refilled his coffee, and watched him eat.

"And it's spreading."

Spreading. He raised an eyebrow.

"Sarah Kay is quieter when she's around you." She swept a hand around, as if brushing out the words. "*Calmer* is more accurate."

Well, that's good, isn't it?

"I think maybe even I am."

Joseph noticed she was sitting perfectly still, as if to convince him of what she'd said. Her chin was on her hand, her elbow on the table, her eyes, unblinking, on his face.

He laid his silverware across his plate, took a sip of coffee, and put the cup down. He rested his hands on the table edge and stared back. He opened one, palm up, pointed, touched his heart. What are you feeling?

Luce ignored the question, as she did sometimes. He was never sure if she'd missed a sign or was simply exerting her right to control the conversation. Everybody, it seemed, assumed that right with him.

She turned the question back. "What are *you* feeling, Joe?"

Sorrow, still, as absurd as that was. Relief, too, that he didn't understand. Something—*someone*—he'd been promised hadn't been delivered. He let his fingers tangle. It's complicated.

"How old was Louise when you knew—what you knew?"

He recognized even as the anger rose in him that it was a wrong response, that she had a terror he couldn't quell, but it came anyway, unbidden, unjustified, unjust. He stood, hoping that would release it, like radiating heat.

"It's like you're *waiting* for something."

Joseph bunched his hands and drove them into his pockets. He shook his head. He pulled his hands out, cupped her ears, and shook his head again. But to himself he thought, *But I am, aren't I?*

"Then what is it?" Her eyes were shiny.

He knew he couldn't tell her even if he could speak. The physics he was a part of was changing.

"I see the two of you talking. You've taught Sarah Kay signs you haven't taught me."

The other way around, Luce. He took his keys from the counter. She's teaching me. *She won't accept silence.*

"Where are you going?"

To work.

"It's Saturday."

I know.

"The party's at five," she said. "Half a dozen kids, and I need your help."

I know that too. He tapped his watch and nodded. I'll be back in time.

"And the adults, after."

Yes.

"Then Louis is taking Sarah Kay trick-or-treating."

I know. I know. I know.

He started the truck up and backed out.

"And it's our anniversary," she said to the retreating truck.

Joseph wound the engine too far on purpose and forced the next gear anyway. He started for the job site out of habit, and kept going even after he'd thought better about it, easing up a little on the speed while he waited for another option to appear, slowing now as he got closer. *I need to go sit on somebody's porch, put my feet up, have a beer, watch a baseball game.*

The thought that had banged around in his head for years finally found its way up again. He pulled a U-turn and steered toward one of the jobs he'd helped with in high school, Heather Lake, sure by now to be soft and green and grown up.

He parked at the edge of the lot farthest from the clubhouse and walked straight across two fairways without looking, daring fate—*no, that's wrong: meeting it*—and crossed to where the chain-link fence kept the kids and houses and yards out. A family barbecue was going on behind him, the dad at the grill, the radio going, the smell of steak making the whole street hungry. Next door a man on a ladder leaned over his gutters. Two boys a couple of houses down were shooting each other with their fingers.

Joseph remembered this edge of the job site, the streets and foundations going in, the machinery parked just there, firing it up when it got light, shutting it down again in the afternoons, remembered sitting on fenders and tailgates and listening to stories until it was nearly dark. Here's where lumber had been stacked like huge bricks under luffing sails of dirty white plastic.

He looked at the fairways he had just crossed and saw under them the hardpan, the topsoil he'd helped haul in, the French drains, the pea rock, the miles of plastic four-inch water pipe, the sprinkler system, and in the air the red dust that in five minutes on a windy day worked itself under the fingernails and into the creases around his ears and eyes, his wrists and neck and elbows.

Out of that busy emptiness that no longer existed Joseph heard "Fore!" and once again turned to watch a golf ball travel in a long, low, lazy-looking arc that headed for a spot between his eyes. Perhaps it was because he crossed them, but before it struck it seemed as if that ball were three or half a dozen, or more than that, all on different trajectories, traveling at different speeds, but they all hit anyway with one impact as they had to.

"Are you all right?"

Waiting for something, Luce had said.

He tried to nod, realized he couldn't because his head and shoulders and the rest of him was on the ground, and got to his feet. He felt his face cautiously, tracing the shape of the knot between his eyes, but his fingers came away without blood. He wasn't dizzy. It barely hurt.

I'm fine.

"Geez, I'm sorry, buddy."

The man doing his gutters had come down from his ladder and curled his fingers through the fence for balance. "Want me to call somebody? An ambulance?"

Joseph shook his head. I'm fine, really. A little boy from the barbecue stared at him wonderingly; the rest of his family had gone inside.

"You sure you're all right?" the man who had hit him asked.

"Find out if he's a lawyer," his partner said, then shut up when he didn't get the laugh he'd hoped for.

"I didn't see you in front of us," the other man said.

Joseph waved that away, pointed to himself. It's okay. My fault. He'd like to see the look on the man's face if he could say, "I did it on purpose."

The group wasn't going to break up on its own, so Joseph walked away. "Geez," he heard the man say, "I think I knocked the talk out of him."

He felt his face again curiously, noting its contours, and was relieved that nothing was dented or broken. He felt light-headed, then corrected that: light-hearted. That golf ball had been hanging in the air for over a decade. And he was surprised to find when he got into the pickup that he had put it in his pocket.

"I might have guessed you'd pick the one day in the year you could raise a bump the size of an egg on your forehead and nobody would notice," Luce said. "How did you do it? It looks like a horn growing."

She'd cleaned the house and dusted the bark of the cedar in the wall, had rehung the false cobwebs and chased the real spiders back into their corners, then had hidden an expensive, fragile thing or two, as Louis was coming.

"Your jobs are all outside, and they're all waiting." She looked at the clock. "Why don't you start with the lights."

She wanted paper lanterns in the trees. He pulled them from their boxes—she'd rented eight long strings—unwound them until they lay straight, then got the construction cord and ladder he'd brought from work last week and put the ladder up against the wall with the tree in it. From this one to another and back would make a long triangle out front. He was supposed to hang others here and there in the branches. He plugged the extension cord in and ran it out a window, knotted the first string into that, and watched it light. Then he carried the new end up, turning on the ladder to see behind and below him as the rest of it followed him up like a paper snake that had just eaten a family of rabbits. All its colors were reflected in the hood of Luce's car.

One by one, he checked the items off his list. When he had finished, he went inside to sit on the sofa for a breather. He caught Luce's attention and put his hand down flat as low as he could: Where's Sarah Kay?

"She's still at Mom's. They'll have her back about three. Wait till you see the costume Mom made for her; she's supposed to be a ghost, but she looks more like a marshmallow."

She pretty much does anyway, Joseph thought.

"I'm still not sure that letting them go alone tonight is a good idea," she said. "He's twice her age."

Joseph nodded.

"Louis is getting into trouble in school, and out of school for that matter, and he looks—"

Like I did as a teenager, Joseph thought.

She wanted to say *unkempt, disreputable,* but that sounded too much like her mother. "Greasy."

Well, that was true.

She sat down next to him on the couch and tilted her head onto his shoulder. "I know we've been through this more than once, honey," she said. "And I know I keep changing sides, but it's not about Louis."

It's not?

"It's not even that he's twelve and Sarah Kay's six. Just six. It's something else, something larger. Or anyway, more complicated."

He waited.

"*I'm* allowed intuition too, aren't I?"

Joseph reached across his own chest and hers and with the fingertips of his left hand touched her temple, where he supposed intuition resided. *We should start counting on yours; mine's gone haywire.*

"I'm not sure we're the ones to give him what he wants from us."

What's that?

"He might be hanging around here, nights, after we're in bed. Not off in the Swamp, but here, at the house."

He sat up, which meant she had to as well. What do you mean?

She looked away, outside. "Footprints in the flower-bed, one right in the middle of my mums. A cigarette butt I turned up, weeding. Who else would it be?"

Louis *had* been around a lot lately. For a while last month Luce had started setting another place at the table, knowing he would happen by for dinner, and then he wouldn't come for three nights, or four, and then he would again. He was having trouble with Mother and Dad and kept threatening to run away. Luce knew all this; perhaps she was afraid that when he did, he'd run away to here.

"It's funny, but I don't mind so much being spied on." Her look, he thought, said differently. "I guess it's the showdown I dread."

Joseph had counted the years and thought he knew what was coming: his father staggering into the house, his face a swirl of colors, saying that Louis had left home, then the call for an ambulance, the surgery. In other little fractured bits of the future he heard his father talking about it to anybody who would listen, mostly when Joseph and Luce and his son—who was his daughter—visited on Sunday afternoons. Sometimes the Searses were invited over too, and his dad and Luke would sit in canvas chairs on the back porch, playing cards and complaining of their infirmities. All this was still clear in his memory of something that hadn't happened yet. Here they were at that time, as near as he could guess from the clues he had, but his dad still had most of his hair and showed no signs of being ill. He remembered, too, putting a hasp on the door. Because of Louis? He'd never seen any future involving him, except perhaps that strange time with all the fires.

He wondered if he even owned a latch. He went out to rummage through the pickup's toolbox, found one, and finished the job he'd started years ago, screwing a hasp into the door's jamb.

Luce watched without comment and when he'd finished pointed at the windows and raised her eyebrows. "You going to drive nails through the sashes too? I thought you liked the door without a lock? I thought that's why you never drilled the hole for one."

He raised his hands—one with the screwdriver still in it—helplessly.

"I wasn't talking about a showdown with Louis. I meant the one with your mother."

I'm really treading water in the deep end here, Luce.

"Why do you suppose he's hanging around here in the dark after we've gone to bed?" She waited and then said to his blank look, "He wants to join a family, Joe, and this is the only one he knows." Joseph started to object, but she didn't let him. "Your mom's lost two of you already. Louise a long time ago. You even earlier. She keeps Louis in the house like it's a cage. Now you want to make this house one too."

He smiled at his wife, and at his daughter playing on the floor with a tea set. He and Luce were invited guests to her tea party and held the tiny cups with their fingernails, but she was ignoring them now in favor of a new arrival: the guest of honor, she had announced, the king of some-place-or-other, her Uncle Louis. Joseph had played that role too, once. Louise at that same age had invited him to those same parties. He was a bit saddened that a year from now he would no longer know what to expect.

Luce's intuition had been exact; Louis came dressed as a cat burglar. In character, he'd noticed the new hasp, walked his fingers along it, and grinned at Luce. "Cool."

Had he winked? They couldn't see his eyes clearly behind the thief's mask, a black scarf he'd cut eyeholes into, folded thin and stretched across the bridge of his nose. Black shoes, black jeans, a black ribbed turtleneck.

He'd sat cross-legged next to Sarah Kay, gravely accepting a cup of tea. "Aren't any other little girls coming?" he asked.

The other little girls arrived soon enough, all in a gaggle, their mothers in tow. Luce brought out the real teacups and poured tea instead of soda. After smiling and nodding and shaking hands, Joseph tried to find a corner to hide in, but one near his brother so he could watch.

Sarah Kay's friends adored Louis, and Joseph thought their mothers did too. Louis made a fuss over each costume: a witch, a princess, an alien, a pirate, a skeleton. *They must have planned this,* Joseph thought, *made calls to find out who's wearing what to the ball.* Sarah Kay was dressed in a billowing white, shapeless affair that looked more like a cloud than the ghost she'd asked for, a stark contrast next to her young uncle.

Listening to his brother's endless, happy chatter, at his funny, ingratiating remarks to the parents, Joseph realized that Louis had received all the articulate wit that had been withheld from him. He wondered if it would do Louis any good.

He watched Luce with the women and admired her ease too, liked the way she guided the conversation from embarrassing, first-day-at-school stories to middle-of-the-night emergencies to imaginative (and from one woman, often alcoholic) recipes for the blinding headaches motherhood is apt to bring. He noticed the way she sat with her back against a swift orange crayon mark that hadn't been on the wall yesterday, and that got him thinking about the small house he'd built with all its imperfections, and he wondered where that put Luce in the hierarchy of wives. *'My husband lectures at the university; what does your husband do?'* He pictured Luce holding her hands at ten and two o'clock, juggling them.

Two of the children couldn't stay long—they had other parties to go to—and when they said their good-byes an hour later, Sarah Kay began to cry and stamp her feet. When the others left too, Luce and Joseph waved from the steps.

"Now what do we do with the kids until dark?" Luce asked out of the side of her mouth.

Louis was standing over Sarah Kay, perplexed at the change in her.

"She's just cranky, honey," Luce said to him. To Joseph she said, "I'd like to get her out of that costume and put her down for an hour, see if she'll take a nap. Can you keep your brother amused for that long?"

She had just gotten her daughter and all that material in her arms when the phone rang. She swept that up too. "Oh, that'll be fine," Luce said, covering the receiver and mouthing, *The party*.

Joseph shrugged.

"No, we're not going to be in costume, but others are coming in them."

Joseph winced.

"Well, no, nothing, I guess."

Joseph sighed.

"See you soon, then," she said, and then, "All right." She hung up and turned to Joseph. "They're coming early. I'm sorry, honey. I'm no good at lying over the phone, and I'm never any good at lying to my mother."

Who else does anybody ever practice on? Joseph wondered as he led his brother outside.

The light, hours still from failing and warm as butter, slanted through the trees horizontally, igniting the few leaves here and there that had begun to turn. The sycamores in the distance rattled with cicadas.

"Nice place," Louis said. "I wonder what Dad's got left to give me?"

The cedars threw shadows so long and thick, the branches of one crossing the trunk of another, it seemed the trees had more lives than one. Joseph walked into them, and Louis followed. Luce, watching from the window of her daughter's room, lost them immediately.

The dusk and silence of the place were at work on Louis, pressing on him like a hand, as Joseph guessed they would, as they did on him, and when he spoke, finally, it was almost in a whisper. "You ever take Louise in here with you?"

Joseph shook his head. *City girl.*

"Mom won't speak of her, ever, and Dad hardly. And *you* can't." He ducked a limb and hurried to draw up beside his brother. He touched Joseph's arm. "She's on my mind a lot lately. I've done the math. I know Mom must've been pregnant with me about the time she died." He pulled his hand back. "That connects the two of us for me."

Within a week, Joseph thought. *Connects which two?*

"She would have graduated last spring."

Joseph was caught by surprise that Louis cared about such things, that he was right, and that Joseph hadn't already thought of it.

"Be out on her own, probably, by now."

Joseph gave him a slow nod: Could be.

"Married, maybe."

Joseph stopped and faced Louis—who backed, surprised, against a sweetgum—opened his palm, pointed, tapped his head. What's on your mind?

"What am I thinking?" He looked down at his black tennis shoes. "I don't know. Sometimes I just get in a hurry." He ripped a piece of bark loose without looking. "Sometimes I need somebody to talk to."

Joseph looked around for a better place to sit, didn't find one, and so leaned against the tree next to Louis's. He tapped his own breastbone.

"All right," Louis said. "Sometimes I want everything at once. A car, a girl, a job, a place of my own."

Joseph nodded.

"I can't wait."

Yes, you can. Waiting is what we're meant to do. Joseph held a hand up, trying to think of a signal, then realized he'd made one.

"You ever see—" his brother began, stopped, then began it again. "You ever see *my* future the way you saw Louise's?"

That's the second time today I've been asked that. Joseph studied the face in front of his, realizing that it was nothing at all like his own, and for the first time in his life lied. *Yes.* And he was glad to see the fear in his brother's eyes.

"What should I do?"

He took his brother's hand, as if Louis were blind. *Live right here,* Joseph said in three deliberate gestures. *In this moment. Now.*

Joseph and Louis walked to the golf-course boundary and then turned back. At the swamp's other edge, where his house sat, where the noise of the party eddied, they stood in the cool air and shadows looking out into sunlight and people and not wanting to join them yet.

Higgerby loomed like a garage sale in front of the barbecue. Over his trousers, half hidden by his sports coat, he wore a plastic grass skirt. The smoke and smell of steaks drifted into the branches.

"I used to be surprised that you've got friends," Louis said.

Me too.

They met Luce's father at the door going out, his stiff leg even stiffer in a cardboard tube, a pegleg. His head was wrapped in a blue paisley bandanna, and underneath a fold of it one of his wife's large gold hoop earrings dangled.

Luce was right behind him. "I wish now I'd put a costume together after all," she whispered to Joseph when Luke and Louis had moved away in opposite directions. "But I couldn't think of how to make you wear one too."

That's all right, Luce; the last time you dressed up for Halloween, you came as a bride.

She was prettier now than when he'd married her, he thought, seeing her in one of those rare moments when she was unaware of him. She had lost a baby, had a baby, wanted another (is *promised* another, he couldn't help but think), and he hoped too that Sarah Kay wouldn't have to grow up alone.

Across the room, Parker raised a beer bottle, and Joseph reluctantly tapped Luce on the hand and went.

Luce's youngest sister, Gail, was tending bar at the kitchen counter, wearing a low-cut, off-the-shoulder peasant blouse that had no reason that he could see to stay on. Her small waist was cinched even tighter with a red sash. At twenty, she still lived with her parents. She was the prettiest of the three Sears daughters, he thought. Joseph, at family gatherings like this one, at picnics, at county fairs, had watched her and had watched other young men watching her, and had seen in their eyes the hopelessness that came over them like a sudden illness when she flicked a strand of hair away from an ear, touched an earring, struck an unconscious pose. She was one of those women who can make men feel lighter just by acknowledging their existence, and because that's all she did, their hearts were cleaved in half.

Louis's was one of those.

Joseph noticed him peripherally, the only unmoving thing in the crowded room, a still, dark spot, a mote in his eye. Joseph pointed to the scotch bottle and the ice bucket, and Gail smiled two smiles and reached two hands for two glasses, and when Joseph looked back two Louises were staring through him at two Gails.

"Something more in it, Joe? Soda? Water?"

Numb, he held the glass with both hands, shook his head, and forced a smile. *This has got to be the end; the present and future are here at the same time.* He excused himself and went to Louis, still standing in the middle of the party like a zombie. Joseph had to touch him to get his attention.

Louis glanced up at him, but his eyes were unfocused. "When did she get so beautiful?"

She's always been beautiful, Louis. *When did you grow up?*

"I think I'm in love."

No need to tell anyone that. You look poleaxed. Joseph poked him in the forehead. *Think.*

Louis *had* been thinking. "We'll be in our twenties together, just barely," he said. "Twenty-one and twenty-nine. I can wait for *that*, I guess."

Joseph poked his own chest with a forefinger. *My* sister. This is *my* family, Louis.

He saw Louis weigh the meaning and understand it, then dismiss it. "What could make us closer than that?"

Luce is right, he thought; *Louis will need a home*—needs one now—*to run to.* He decided to take the hasp off tonight as soon as the guests left.

"I think I'll get a soda," Louis said, and winked. "If she's the one handing those out too?"

Joseph looked at him sternly for a moment but had to grin in spite of his double vision. He nodded.

"See you."

Joseph wished again he'd owned that sort of confidence at that age; he'd been *certain* at twelve of any number of things, all of which had filled him with terror, all of them driven by fear. But lately even that certainty, horrible as it was, had deserted him. He watched Louis slide between the guests, each with a shadow-self, half expecting to see his brother lift his hand and pick a pocket.

Gail was now handing out drinks to a crowd of men (only three, but nine or a dozen), one or two or three of them a figure that he only belatedly recognized as his father, and then only because of the way he brushed Louis away from him, and Louis went. When he turned, the colors in his face were too familiar. Pink and yellow and blue.

His dad saw him, after following Louis's trail back to the starting point, and came over. "Happy anniversary, Son. Seven's the Itch. What's that bump between your eyes? You growing another one?"

Joseph could only stare. His father wore a skullcap that he hadn't pulled down tightly enough, so it wrinkled and bagged. A few stray plastic hairs like wires looked as if they might fall into his drink. His eyes were rimmed in something dark—eyebrow pencil, Joseph imagined—and he'd shaded the natural hollows of his face to make it look gaunt. The swirl of color in his face was hideous.

He laughed at Joseph's look, and it turned into a rasping cough. "I know, I know; you want to know who I am. Well, I'm no one special—not a movie or cartoon character. I'm just a dead man left out in the heat of the swamp too long." He raised his glass, as if saluting dead men everywhere. Or heat, or swamps. He looked as if he'd already saluted a couple of times this afternoon. "And anyway, your mother didn't dress up, so I thought I should."

Joseph's knees were loose, and he managed the six steps it required to get to a chair, but when he turned to sit his father had turned too and was slipping back into the crowd as if sliding underwater.

Instead of sitting, he made his way outside to the air, to the table farthest from the house. He parted the guests like a drunk, dodging their ghosts but stumbling into real people. Luce had turned the lanterns on, and they glowed nicely above the yard and here and there, like Christmas, in the trees. *They're prettier like this,* he thought; *twice as many as he had strung.* He felt as if his heart would burst in confusion and joy.

Higgerby, as if smelling it, joined him. He put his drink down on the oilcloth and spread his round hands flat on the table for leverage. "Now, then," he said, sitting heavily.

He doesn't wear any rings, Joseph thought. *And there are two Higgerbys, really; a younger one trapped inside this one.*

"Are you still getting a look at what's ahead?"

Joseph sat too, still with the picture of his father in his mind. When was the last time he'd seen a future that had actually arrived? Louise's death. That ax. The golf ball from this morning that he'd nearly given up on, that he'd had to go and find. *What else?* All those pictures that he knew couldn't be real. He shook his head.

"No? The screamer doesn't either. In fact—"

The door to the house was swept open and his mother, holding Sarah Kay, stood outlined against the house's glare. The angle he had of them made it look as if his daughter's costume were on his mother's shoulders.

"Joseph?" she called, shading her eyes.

"I'll come back later," Higgerby said. He put his glass down in the bull's-eye on the table, and when he rose to go Helen found him.

"How can you do this?" she asked, halfway across the yard.

Do what?

His wife appeared at the door and started down. *Like targets in a shooting gallery,* Joseph thought. *Dad's next.*

Luce was running now to catch Helen. The guests had gathered in a knot just inside the house and the open door, Louis's slim black shape among them.

"She's upset at Sarah Kay's costume," Luce called to him over his mother's shoulder.

Helen turned to Luce, right behind her, and Luce's heels scored the dirt to keep from running her over.

"Upset?" It sounded almost quizzical.

"I didn't mean anything, Helen. Sarah Kay chose a costume, and my mother made it for her."

"You didn't mean anything?"

His father, as Joseph had guessed he would, was making his way across the yard. His mother-in-law started down too, but somebody—Luke, he thought—pulled her back. Sarah Kay, in her grandmother's arms, signaled to Joseph, *I'm scared*, and began to cry.

As if from a distance, as if from a great height, he saw his family—his mother and daughter in front of him, Luce just behind them, his father behind her, and Louis, still trapped in the house—stretched like beads on a string. The multiple, synchronous images snapped back into one with a click he could hear.

"Don't you see?" Helen asked him, turning Sarah Kay's wet face with her hand.

Joseph got up and gently took Sarah Kay from his mother's arms, and she clung, whistled softly at him like a night bird, tapped on his wrist, *Don't put me down.*

"Let's all sit down," his father said, pulling out one of the picnic benches. "Helen?"

But his mother wouldn't sit. She swung her right arm in a gesture, her left one locked against her side as if it still held a little girl. "We get together two or three times a year, for one holiday or another, or they come to our place, and all of us get along. We like each other, don't we?"

Luce nodded, beginning to cry too, but Helen wasn't looking in her direction. She was staring at her husband, who was watching the ice move in his drink. "Don't they know my little girl is still here?" She laid a hand on her breast and turned back to Joseph. "Don't they remember what happened?"

"We do remember, Mom," Luce said.

"Do you?"

Joseph knew she did. Luce had watched the long-haired boy who would become her husband stand for a moment on the tiles in nothing but his briefs before diving into the pool's lit depths. She'd seen the bottom of one foot, bloody from kicking in the fence, disappearing under the reflection. She'd seen him come up again, his face a sheet of bubbles, treading water with his limp sister in his arms.

"You're making too much of this, Helen."

"*Too* much, Frank?"

"It's okay, Dad," Luce said. "She's right."

"I don't need you defending me." Helen's eyes stabbed for a second, looking through her, but softened as if she recognized her own eyes in Luce's face. "Oh, honey, I'm sorry." She took a step toward her and stopped. "I—I—"

Sarah Kay wriggled from her seat in Joseph's arms and ran to the cedar in the wall of the house, where a lantern dangled.

"That's hot, honey," Helen said sharply.

"Helen."

She looked at her husband, at her son, at her granddaughter, at her daughter-in-law. Her eyes filled, but she wiped them with the heels of her hands and finally smiled, looking at her palms as if something were written there. "It's just that she looks so much like Louise," she said, and walked a little unsteadily to where Sarah Kay crouched, and picked her up.

But she's not.

A trembling started in his mother's feet, as if the ground were shaking, but she steadied herself. "Who are you trick-or-treating with tonight?" she asked Sarah Kay.

"Uncle Louis."

His mother stared first at Joseph. "You're not really going to let her go alone?" Then she wheeled to ask Luce, "Are you?"

"Not alone," Luce said. "With Louis."

"We don't even want *Louis* out at night. He's only twelve."

"Helen."

"Is this your doing, Frank?"

"Louis isn't Louise either," Luce said, "any more than Sarah Kay is."

"Don't you see?" his mother asked. She looked again at each of them separately, squeezing Sarah Kay more tightly. Her fingers went to her throat, to the pearls she wore that Sarah Kay was holding on to. "We'll come apart if we don't take care."

I've lived like that, Mother; it doesn't work.

The day was gone, turning dark for real. Louis and Sarah Kay shifted from foot to foot in the crowd of adults, eager to be off. "We need to be going, Daddy. Can I go, *please?* It's safe, I *promise. Believe* me."

If Joseph thought for an instant that his daughter knew that for sure, that her promise carried any conviction he needed to heed, he'd shake until he couldn't stop, until the parts inside came unstuck for good. But he didn't believe it, so after glancing at his wife and getting her nod, he motioned for them to go.

He followed them as far as the front steps. The first bright stars were up, the benign ones, drawn like insects to the moon. At only a short distance in the late dusk, in their costumes of thief and ghost, Louis holding a paper bag for his loot, Sarah Kay gripping a plastic jack-o-lantern with both tiny hands, they reminded him of the bride and groom on top of a wedding cake. Luce patted his hand, then took it in hers. Joseph watched until they had grown indistinct and thought, *If they'd just turn around they'd see me and Luce in the wedge of light the house casts, see our hands raised, saying, Stop, Go, I love you, Come back, Take care, Good-bye. Go on.*